A CAPTAIN DARES . . .

"Your position right at this moment, Caroline, is in my arms. And when I hold a beautiful young woman in my arms, and she's not there for dancing with, then I reckon there's only one thing left to do."

And suiting the action to the word, he once more pressed his warm, firm mouth against hers, holding her so close against his hard, lean body that she had no breath to protest.

Caroline's head was whirling with any number of things she felt beholden to say. But all she could manage to splutter was: "A gentleman would never have dreamed of doing such a thing!"

He raised her hand to his lips and said, "That's where you're wrong, ma'am. A gentleman would have dreamed of doing it, but only a man would have done it."

The Reckless Wager

Nella Benson

THE RECKLESS WAGER

A Bantam Book / August 1980

ISBN 0-553-13973-8

Bantam Books are published by Bantam Books, Inc. Its trademark, consisting of the words "Bantam Books" and the portrayal of a bantam, is Registered in U.S. Patent and Trademark Office and in other countries. Marca Registrada. Bantam Books, Inc., 666 Fifth Avenue, New York, New York 10103.

PRINTED IN THE UNITED STATES OF AMERICA

0 9 8 7 6 5 4 3 2 1

For Susan and Michael

1

A brisk autumn breeze whipped the crisp yellowing leaves into a series of miniature whirlwinds and sent them spiralling across the cobbled roadway. Just then a bright, sporty-looking phaeton swung smartly round the curve of the crescent, scattering a cloud of them in all directions. A sprinkling of their dusty flakes settled on the crooked figure of a knife grinder sitting aside the wooden saddle of his small handcart at the edge of the curb. With an impatient gesture he brushed them away and once more set the wheel of his grindstone in motion against a steel blade. The little tweeny, who had just finished sweeping the black-and-white-marble tiles in the portico of Walford House, watched despairingly as the draft from the carriage wheels carried the pile of leaves at her feet back across the grey stone steps. She heaved a sigh of resignation, and blowing the frill of her mobcap from her forehead, patiently retraced her steps to begin her task all over again.

But the young woman glaring down on this little scene from one of the long windows of the upstairs drawing room showed no sign of interest. Normally she would have been intrigued with the comings and goings in the busy London street below, having precious little else to do with her time. Today, however, her deep amber-coloured eyes flashed more brightly than the steel against the grinder's stone. And the white delicately boned hand holding a riding crop flicked it angrily against her heavy dark green velvet skirt.

Miss Eliza Fairchild glanced up from the fine piece of lace she was engaged in making. "Don't do that, Caroline," she reproved her niece in a gentle voice. "It makes you look like a spoiled child. And were anyone to see you, it would give a totally erroneous impression."

Caroline, her bronze hair glinting in the midmorning sunlight, flung round in response to the rebuke. "Well, you just can't do it, Aunt Eliza. I won't let you," she exploded.

Fortunately for all concerned, Lady Caroline Fairchild, whose fiery temper well matched the colour of her hair, rarely gave vent to it. On the rare occasions that she did so, it set everyone in a pother. The servants scurried away quickly to find themselves a job at a distance, while the duchess invariably dissolved into an attack of the vapours and the duke hastily left for Brooks with instructions not to expect him back until late.

There was only one person who always remained cool, calm, and collected under the onslaught of Caroline's wrath, and that was Eliza, the duke's younger sister. "Oh, but I can, my dear. I do not have to ask your permission, and my mind is fully made up on the matter." There was a quiet note of determination in the gentle voice, and it called Caroline to her senses.

From the day when, as a small child, her home had been invaded by her uncle and his family upon his inheriting the title, her aunt had been the only one who could manage her. She had exercised a firm but kind authority over the little girl who had been so tragically orphaned when her parents had been drowned returning from a visit to the New World.

Caroline had soon learned that she could either bully or wheedle her uncle into giving in to her, but Aunt Eliza was someone to contend with. She had never wavered either in her warm affection or her firm intention when it came to dealing with her spirited young niece. Which was the reason Caroline loved and respected her more than anyone else in the world.

"But, Aunt Eliza, you can't go all that way. Why, it's at the other end of the earth. You must stay here and look after me." Her peremptory tone masked a note of pleading that betokened her true feelings.

Her aunt folded her work up into a neat little bundle, and getting up from her high-backed chair, crossed over to the sewing table to put it away before answering her niece. She was an attractive woman in her early forties, and although her hair beneath the little lace cap was almost grey, it had once been as bronze as Caroline's, and her eyes were the same deep golden brown. In fact, they were very much alike, which was why she was sharing her niece's present emotions, although she expressed them in a different way.

She joined her young charge by the window, and taking the girl's hand in her own, led her over to where a bright fire crackled cheerfully in the hearth. "What you really mean to say, Caroline, is that you would prefer that I did not go because you will miss me, and I can well understand that." She gave a slight sigh as she drew Caroline down into the little chair beside her own.

"Believe me, my dear, this has not been an easy decision for me to make. But your Uncle Stephen needs me—"

"So do I!" her niece wailed.

"Not in the same way, and I'm quite sure that it will not be very long now before you marry and become mistress of your own household. On the other hand, your uncle is now a widower with a young family to bring up, and he sadly needs the help that only a woman can give him."

"Well, I think that it is very selfish of him to even have suggested it. He chose to go and live all those miles away in Canada, and now he expects you to give up everything here and go and live amongst those . . . those savages!" her niece replied hotly.

Her aunt gave a gay little laugh. "In the first place, my dear, from all accounts they are very far from savages in York Town. And in the second place, apart from your company, what am I giving up here?"

Caroline looked across at her aunt, a puzzled expression in her eyes. "But aren't you happy here? This is your home."

Her aunt shook her head. "No, this is a house in which I am permitted to live under the protection of my brother and at the whim of his wife. I am not needed here; nobody will miss me when I have gone. If anything, I expect they will be only too pleased to see the back of me, although your uncle made some mild protest when I told him of my decision."

"But what of me? I shall miss you terribly."

"Yes, I'm sure you will. But perhaps my going will help you to make up your mind to accept the hand of one of your many suitors. It is high time you did so."

"What makes you so certain I will marry? Hannah tells me you had plenty of admirers when you were my age, but you never chose to marry any of them."

"Hannah has no right to gossip so much," her aunt replied. "If she hadn't been with me for so many years, I would seriously think of reprimanding her. Incidentally, she has agreed to go to Canada with me. In spite of her many tiresome ways, I find that very good of her. It means that she will probably never see any of her kith and kin again."

"Oh, so you are not only going to leave me, you are also

going to take the only trustworthy servant in the family, as well." Caroline tossed back the curls that had tumbled down over her high forehead. "But that is neither here nor there. You haven't answered my question."

"What was it, dear? I'm afraid I've forgotten."

Caroline viewed her aunt with suspicion. She had the distinct feeling that Miss Fairchild was evading the issue. "I asked you why it should be any easier for me to find a suitable husband than it was for you."

"There are many reasons, my dear, not least amongst them that you are the most eligible young heiress in the *haut ton,* whereas I was merely the youngest of five daughters and three sons. When it came to my turn, my expectations were exceedingly small."

Caroline gave a little snort of disgust. "This marriage mart sickens me. No one spoke for you because you didn't have enough money, and I'm afraid that they only want me because I have so much. It's all so ridiculous and it quite bores me."

Eliza gave one of her slow, sad smiles. "You won't always find it so. When the right man comes along, your heart will tell you, and you won't care whether he has a penny or a pound, believe me."

"You sound as though you speak from experience, aunt, yet I have never heard tell that there was anyone special in your life," Caroline said curiously.

"That's because nobody ever knew about him," her aunt replied. "He was a young naval officer from a family of little importance. He had spent what money he had buying his commission, so we decided to wait until he returned from the wars. . . ." A tear trickled down her cheek and she made haste to brush it away, but not before Caroline had noticed it.

"And he didn't come back?" she asked softly.

Eliza shook her head. "No, he was killed during the battle of the Nile while serving under Admiral Nelson. But that was a long time ago," Eliza said, brightening up; she was not one to indulge in self-pity. "And now that that wretched little Corsican has been finally defeated, I'm sure there are a great number of perfectly splendid young men for you to choose from."

"Like Sir D'Arcy Letton?" Caroline said mischievously, hoping to bring some colour back into her aunt's cheeks. She knew Eliza detested the man and the mere mention of his name would spark a response.

"You know perfectly well what opinion I hold of D'Arcy Letton. I cannot think why you continue to encourage him."

"If I were to tell you that I was thinking of accepting his most recent proposal, would you consider staying in England to try to dissuade me?" Caroline continued her teasing.

"No, I would not!" her aunt exclaimed indignantly. "In fact, I would feel so completely dispirited at my failure to inculcate at least a glimmer of common sense into that pretty head of yours, I should pack up and leave the house immediately. That man is an out-and-out rogue, and if it were not for his connections with the prince and his coterie, he would not be allowed in polite society at all. As it is, he is only tolerated."

"Oh, come now, aunt, you are being a trifle hard on him. He is acknowledged to be one of the best-looking men in the *ton*, with his dark hair and audacious manner—"

"And his wicked, bold eyes," her aunt interrupted. "And I for one consider his manners outrageous rather than merely audacious. If I didn't credit you with a great deal of common sense, I wouldn't have a moment's peace whenever you go out with him. I suppose that is where you have been this morning, riding in the Row with him?"

"Yes, as a matter of fact it is." Caroline had regained her good humour and was enjoying a verbal sparring match with her aunt. "That was when he made his seventh—or was it his eighth?—proposal . . . I've quite lost count." She got up and waltzed over to her aunt's sewing table and hunted for the little bag of homemade peppermints that she knew was always hidden there. Popping one into her mouth, she said, "I've told him that I may give him my answer when he comes to pay his respects to you and the duchess this afternoon. It is today, your 'at home,' isn't it?"

"Yes, it is," Eliza answered tartly. "But now you've told me that, I don't think I will stay at home. Really, Caroline, I do wish you wouldn't see or be seen so much with that young man. It can only harm your reputation. He never has a good word to say for anybody, and those who fetch gossip will also carry it. I'm quite certain that he goes away and tells the most outrageous stories about you." The colour had returned to her aunt's face with a vengeance. The poor lady looked quite put about.

Caroline was quick to reassure her. "Don't fadge yourself, aunt. I know what he's like, but he's much more fun than those other milksops that come to pay court. It adds some spice to life just battling with him." It was her turn to sigh wistfully. "Heaven alone knows, life is boring enough, and without D'Arcy to wrangle with, I truly don't know how I would pass the time. After a while this continuous round of the London season, followed by hunting and the country for Christmas, with perhaps a trip to Bath on the side, becomes more than I can tolerate. If there wasn't someone like him around to make me laugh, I would go out of my mind."

Eliza's lips had been twitching with amusement as she watched her niece dramatize the boredom of the *beau monde*. But her face took on a sterner expression as she spoke. "That is exactly why it is high time you found yourself a husband and settled down to bring up a brood of happy children in your own home." Caroline started to repeat her remarks about the suitability, or rather the lack of it, amongst the young bucks of her acquaintance, but her aunt silenced her.

"No, Caroline, I want you to listen to me seriously for a moment. It is something that has been on my mind for a long time, and now that I am going away, I must speak of it. Come and sit down again, I want to have a heart-to-heart with you."

Caroline meekly obeyed. It wasn't often that her aunt lectured her, which is what she meant by a heart-to-heart, and when she did, she always had something of import to say.

"You are twenty-one, and I would give you two, perhaps three years at the very most, and that only because of your fortune . . . . Certainly by the time you are twenty-five you will notice the change. A new generation of young men and women will have come along to take your place. Invitations to assemblies and house parties will gradually become fewer, because you will be the odd one out. The others in your set will have married and you will be too old for the new one. Then, do you know what will happen?" She paused to allow her next words to sink in. "One day you will discover that you are expected to wear a little lace cap and shawl and take your place in the household of the nearest male relative, who will offer you his protection. You will become a spinster aunt, who will help to supervise the staff, help with the bringing up of children who are not your own, and do all the chores of a hostess without any of the privileges that go with it. If you are invited to dinner, it will be merely to make up the numbers. At house parties, it will only be as an afterthought because someone has suggested that you might be useful to stay with the children while the others go out. So don't you make a mistake in thinking that life will always be as boring as you find it today. In a few years' time it will become very much worse unless you make up your mind to do something about it very soon."

Caroline bent down to throw another log on the fire. Suddenly she felt as though the room had grown chilly. She put it down to the fact that she was beginning to cool off after her ride in the brisk autumn air. But her aunt's words had found their mark. Eliza had only voiced the thoughts that had been lurking at the back of her own mind.

"There, I feel much better now that I have spoken what was on my mind. And perhaps you will find it easier to understand why I have decided to accept Stephen's invitation to go to Canada. For twenty years that has been the story of my life, and like you, I am heartily bored with it. I don't expect life will be as easy there as it is here, but that in itself will be a challenge. And if I don't grasp this opportunity, I shall have to reconcile myself to sitting in a corner crocheting away the rest of my life. For after you have gone, there will be nothing else left for me."

Caroline felt her own eyes pricking with tears as she remembered how her aunt had always been so ready and willing to help her plan for all the parties and visits that are the delight of a young girl's life. And how she had sat and listened for hours to all the chitchat concerning them. Never once had she given any indication that her own life was full of boredom.

"Oh, Aunt Eliza, what a selfish wretch I've been. I don't deserve anyone like you to care for me. All I've ever thought about has been my own enjoyment. But if only you will stay, I will make it up to you, truly I will," Caroline pleaded.

Eliza Fairchild leant forward and patted her niece's hand. "Now you're not to talk like that. If it hadn't been for you, my life would have been much duller. Although you can be willful on occasion and you must watch that temper of yours, you have a kind heart, so you're not to reproach yourself. As to making it up to me, my dear, that is beyond your capabilities. There are certain rigidly proscribed rules for society, and unfortunately, we all have to abide by them."

"Well, I think that it is crazy, and we should alter them. It often makes me angry when I'm told, 'Oh, you can't do that . . . it's not ladylike.' Only the other day D'Arcy was saying how people gossip about me because I insist on riding with the hounds instead of following genteelly in a carriage. I'm not going to be shut in like a pampered lapdog and not do the things I like just because society frowns on them. Who makes all these rules anyway?"

"D'Arcy and his like," her aunt replied promptly. "Oh, he may appear to agree with you now. But I guarantee that the moment you married him he would hedge you in with all kinds of restrictions, and the law is on his side. You must keep in mind, my dear, that once you are married, you and your entire fortune become your husband's property. And unless you conform to his wishes, he can make life very unhappy for you—even to the extent of forbidding you access to your own children."

Caroline tossed her head angrily. "And you want me to marry. Why, I think I would be better off to stay an old maid."

"No, Caroline. Just be careful in your choice of a husband, and D'Arcy Letton is not that man, believe me."

"Oh, I do, aunt. I realize what he is like, but I find his company amusing, and he does treat me as though I have a spark of sense instead of simpering around paying me quite ridiculous compliments and quizzing me through a spyglass. Anyway, enough of me. If you are quite set on going to Upper Canada, when do you plan to leave?" Caroline tried to sound enthusiastic about her aunt's plans, although her own heart was heavy at the thought of her going.

"As soon as the weather permits after Christmas. Stephen suggests that I try to time it so that I arrive in York Town about the middle of April. By then the weather will be improving, and if the winter hasn't been too severe, most of the snow will have disappeared. That will give me the summer to get settled in."

"York Town! I thought the Americans had pretty well destroyed it when they occupied it in 1813?"

"No, the fort and government buildings were either burned during the fighting or set to the torch later, but most of the houses came through unscathed. And Stephen tells me all that unpleasantness is behind them now, and the capital is growing rapidly. The population has more than doubled in the past three years, and with the officers and men at the garrison, there is somewhere in the neighbourhood of three thousand people there, apart from the settlers up in the bush."

"But what will you do with yourself all day? You'll be

bored to tears with only soldiers and Indians to talk to."

"Nonsense, Caroline, I've told you the place is now quite civilized. Why, they have an assembly at the garrison at least twice a week. Then there are the lieutenant governor and his lady, and the wives of the officials. Besides which, from all accounts, I shall have much more to do with the housekeeping. Apparently there is a great dearth of servants over there. As soon as they arrive, they discover a new sense of freedom and take off into the hinterland to build their own little farms. That is why I'm so grateful that Hannah has agreed to come with me."

Caroline laughed gaily. "I think you are quite safe with dear old Hannah. I can't see her as a settler's wife, she is far too fond of her comforts."

"Aren't we all?" her aunt replied. "But don't let us talk about that. I'm quite all right just so long as I think of the town, but it is when my mind starts dwelling upon those vast forests and whatever creatures they hide in them that my courage begins to fail me."

"Never; courage is one thing you'll never lack." Caroline glanced up at the stately grandfather clock in the corner. "Great Jehoshaphat! Just look at the time, and I haven't changed yet." She gave her aunt an affectionate peck on her cheek and hurried off to get dressed for the afternoon's "at home."

Caroline rang for her maid to come and help her dress. She decided to wear a pretty sprigged muslin with narrow frills around the sleeves, which flattered her shapely hands. Although she had many attributes that the other girls in her set would have given much to possess, her hands were her major vanity, and Caroline knew how to use them to the greatest advantage. It was for that reason, as much as any other, that she had spent tedious hours practicing her music. Where better, than at the piano or harp, could she display them and elicit such compliments?

When Martha had finished dressing her hair, she went downstairs to partake of a light lunch with her two aunts. The duchess, of course, was related only by marriage. She was a silly, empty-headed little woman whose moods ranged from indignation at an imagined slight to persistent attacks of the vapours. Which only meant that she had an excuse to retire to her room with the latest novel and indulge herself with chocolates. Caroline had given up trying to hold an intelligent conversation with her a long time ago. But now, as she sat listening to the duchess chattering away to Aunt Eliza, she wondered how she would exist when there was no one else to make a diversion. The prospect of having to try to keep up a polite chitchat with her ladyship was dismal indeed.

Luncheon having finished, Caroline retired to her room and sat at the window until it was time for the carriages to arrive. She delayed joining the party that was assembling downstairs for as long as politeness would allow, but finally good manners demanded that she put in an appearance.

Immediately she made her entrance into the big salon, she was surrounded by the usual coterie of admirers, all of them intent on impressing her with their latest feats with the horses or at the gambling tables. They had learned by now that they would quickly lose Caroline's attention if they spent the time paying her idle compliments. Even so, she was heartily pleased when D'Arcy Letton arrived. He was not at all popular with the majority of young men who attended on the duchess and her niece. He was more at home with the fashion-conscious young bucks that surrounded the prince regent. Furthermore, he had a quick wit that too often verged on spite and had an uncommon knack of making others appear foolish. So as soon as he joined Lady Caroline, the company began to melt away, having little hope of competing with him for her attention.

"What an utterly boring crowd they are," he drawled. "If it weren't for you, my dear Caroline, I vow I wouldn't waste a moment in their company. Why, the only bright spot in an otherwise dull afternoon is the news that your aunt, Miss Fairchild, is intending to leave us for the wilds of Canada." He gave his usual rather high-pitched laugh, which suddenly grated on Caroline's ears.

"And pray, sir, why should that cause you so much amusement?" she asked coldly.

D'Arcy remembered in what esteem she held Miss Fairchild. "Oh, upon my word, Lady Caroline, you didn't think that I was laughing at Miss Eliza? Never! She is quite one of the worthiest ladies of my acquaintance. It is only that I find the thought of such a genteel lady of Miss Fairchild's sensibilities descending upon those illiterate colonials highly amusing. But she is of such excellent virtue that I'm sure she will prove a softening and refining influence for them."

"And what call have you for labelling them illiterate, Sir D'Arcy? You seem to forget that my Uncle Stephen is one of their number."

D'Arcy Letton knew he had offended her, and though he was far too proud and conceited to apologize, he did his best to make amends. "My dear Lady Caroline, forgive me, but one swallow does not a summer make, and all that. And while I am the first to admit that your uncle is an admirable man, he is the exception that proves the rule."

"You speak with great authority, Sir D'Arcy. Would you care to tell me how you came by such intimate knowledge both of my uncle and of the society of Upper Canada in general?"

"Certainly. It was my misfortune to be garrisoned at York during our war with those wretched Yankees. The place is a wilderness. No one in his right mind would stay to change horses, let alone settle there. And I may say that without giving further offense, for I too have relatives there."

"Really!" Caroline's tone was icy. She looked up into D'Arcy's dark, handsome face and noted for the first time how weak his chin was.

"Yes, my cousin John Kendall has recently moved his family there from the east coast, where they had settled with other loyalists. I was never greatly impressed by Cousin John's intelligence, which only goes to confirm my opinion of the people who choose to settle there."

"I am beginning to realize that you tend to take a very jaundiced view of the world, as you rarely have a good word to say for anyone." The amber eyes were flashing, but the sight of them only amused D'Arcy and made him press the attack. He liked his women to have some fire to them, as he did his horses; it was all the sweeter breaking them. And he was determined that Lady Caroline Fairchild would one day become his wife, by fair means or foul.

"I speak nothing more than the truth, Caroline," he replied, dropping into the audacious habit he had of calling her by her first name without using her title. "I am so sure of what I say that I am willing to wager my entire fortune that you would not be able to stand the place for a year. Apart from anything else, the climate and conditions would be far too hard for a lady of your delicate upbringing."

He spoke with such insolent confidence that Caroline's temper reached boiling point. "Done," she said quickly, and seeing the startled look on D'Arcy's face, decided to give him no opportunity to back down. Turning to the assembled company, she said in a loud voice, "Ladies and gentlemen, I would like you to bear witness to a wager I have just made with Sir D'Arcy Letton. His fortune against mine that I will not go to Canada with my aunt and stay there for one whole year—I believe that was the time limit you set?" She turned back to Letton, who had quickly recovered his poise.

Eliza Fairchild, who had risen hurriedly from her chair at Caroline's announcement, said firmly, "Caroline, young ladies do not gamble and no gentleman would expect them to." She turned and glowered at D'Arcy.

"This is one occasion when you will have to overlook the niceties, for I have already accepted, and I will not have it said that I did not honour my debts," Caroline replied.

"I'm afraid that is true, Miss Fairchild, the wager was agreed upon even before the terms had been finalized. But of course, if Lady Caroline wishes to reconsider, I would not be so ungallant as to hold her to it. She is, after all, one of the weaker sex." His dark eyes glinted maliciously; he had seen how the situation might be turned to his advantage and was now determined to provoke Caroline into going through with it.

Caroline tossed her head. "I have already said the bargain has been made. And no matter what your terms, you will not win, so they are of little consequence."

"Then I will wager my entire fortune against your hand in marriage that you will not stay in York Town for a year and a day."

A stifled gasp went up from the company, and several of the ladies hurriedly began fluttering their fans, while the duchess called for her smelling salts.

Caroline's fiery confidence had suddenly cooled at the mention of the word "marriage." If it were only her fortune at stake, she was sure she could manage without it if necessary. But under his terms, D'Arcy would not only gain control of her money but she would be tied to him for life. She realized now just what a soundrel he was, but there was little she could do, for everyone's eyes were upon her.

Her cheeks were flushed, and she felt her hands beginning to tremble. She looked across at her Aunt Eliza, hoping to draw strength from her, but for once the poor lady looked quite distraught. Caroline rose from her chair and with all the dignity she could muster held out her hand to Sir D'Arcy. "I accept," she said. "Although I prefer that the sacrament of marriage should not be treated like money at a gaming table. However, as I have said, it is of no consequence, for I am quite made up to stay in Canada for a year and a day. Who knows," she added with a deliberate lightness, "I may even decide to settle there for life. In which case, Sir D'Arcy, I shall expect you to make the necessary arrangements to have your fortune transferred to my Uncle Stephen's keeping in Canada. Unless, of course, I have found myself a husband from amongst the savages." And with a gay little laugh she tapped Letton playfully on the arm and swept out of the room.

Upstairs in her own bedchamber, Caroline let the tears flow. She could hear the carriages hastening away and knew the entire company would be hurrying to spread the news of the wager. By tonight there would not be one person of any account who would not know about it.

"Oh, my dear child, what have you done? I knew one day that temper of yours would get you into trouble." Her aunt bustled into the room, her expression full of concern. "And that wretched man, so ready to take advantage of you. Do you know what the duchess has just told me?"

Caroline shook her head. "No, but nothing would surprise me this afternoon." She did her best to appear nonchalant and not let her aunt know the cold fear that clutched her.

"Why, someone was telling her that D'Arcy Letton is in desperate straits, having gambled away all his own money and most of his expectations from his uncle the Duke of Blaise. Even if you should win the wager, I doubt if there will be anything but a mountain of debts."

"Well, no matter. I was already of a mind to accompany you, for I am heartily bored, as I told you."

"Yes, but it is one thing for me to go at my age and with the knowledge that I can always return home if I find the circumstances too vexing. But now, no matter what, you will have to stay there or return home and spend the rest of your life with D'Arcy Letton."

"Then that settles it, doesn't it, Aunt Eliza? I shall just have to make up my mind that, come what may, I will stay there. But as you have every intention of doing so, I see no reason to suppose that I will fail, for after all, I shall have you as my guide and mentor."

"That will be a constant delight to me," her aunt said, giving her an affectionate hug. "But as to my being your guide, if the truth be known, I'm terrified at the prospect, so it will be a case of the blind leading the blind. I only hope that dear Stephen keeps an adequate staff, especially as it appears that his position necessitates his entertaining quite frequently."

The prospect of the exciting new life ahead of her quite took the sting out of D'Arcy Letton's wager. Besides, not for one moment did Caroline doubt that she would win. The next few weeks were filled with preparations for the voyage; Aunt Eliza kept referring to it as their "great adventure."

Much of their time was spent with the dressmakers and milliners, for both ladies were determined to arrive with their wardrobes in the very latest style. They had no doubt at all that the colonials would be quite behind the times in that respect. Apart from the major problem of keeping abreast of the London fashions, neither of them was concerned, for they were certain their lives would vary little from the normal round to which they were accustomed. Eliza Fairchild *was* a trifle concerned about some of the items that her brother had suggested they should bring with them, particularly as he laid great emphasis on lotions, ointments, and sundry drugs. He also told them to make sure they had several pairs of stout boots and some woollen socks, the mere thought of which sent both ladies into a state of shock.

Sir D'Arcy Letton was singularly unhelpful when it came to answering their questions as to the conditions they might expect. No doubt because he had no intention of assisting Caroline to win the wager. However, he did give them some very useful hints on how they might make their journey more congenial, and for those they were eternally grateful.

2

It was a blustery day in mid-January when the two ladies embarked on the *Daisy Belle,* a trim schooner sailing from Liverpool to New York. As well as their sea chests and sundry other baggage, they had followed D'Arcy Letton's advice that they should also provision themselves. The food provided by the shipping company was not only often indifferent but also frequently ran short before the end of the voyage, especially if the ship should be delayed by bad weather.

They, of course, were cabin passengers, and Miss Eliza Fairchild was quite enchanted to find the walls oak-lined and the furnishings simple but adequate. She had envisioned herself having to sleep in a hammock. Lady Caroline, on the other hand, was rather put out to discover that they would have to share it with Hannah, but was soon reconciled to the idea when she discovered that the only alternative was for their maid to share the terrible conditions of a steerage passage with a crowd of verminous immigrants. As it happened, it turned out for the best, as her aunt suffered severely from *mal de mer* and Caroline was mightily relieved to have faithful Hannah always at hand.

The first two weeks out from port were cold but pleasant. But by the time they reached mid-Atlantic the weather became quite rough and squally, as did the tempers of both passengers and crew. Eliza refused to leave the cabin, and Caroline did so only to take a constitutional around the deck each day. On these occasions one or other of the young officers invariably made it his business to accompany her. She welcomed both their company and their protection, for the manners of the immigrants and crew left much to be desired. Although the steerage passengers were not allowed on the main deck, some of the bolder ones would frequently find their way there, and their remarks were often unseemly and insulting.

Once or twice the ladies invited the captain or one of his senior officers to their cabin for a game of cards, but neither Eliza nor her niece would encourage them to become too familiar. It was well recognized that although the British seamen had proved themselves invincible during the recent wars, socially they were considered far below the status of the army officers. Otherwise the ladies whiled away the time reading their stock of novels by Walter Scott. Stephen Fairchild had mentioned that although there was a library in York Town, it had as yet only one of the famous author's works, so they had come well prepared.

Returning from her brief walk one day, Caroline was happy to be able to reassure her aunt that they were making good time. The captain had told her that if luck remained on their side, they should reach New York by early March. They had followed Mr. Fairchild's advice and chosen that route rather than travelling via Quebec and Montreal, which would take longer. Also they might well be delayed if the ice on the St. Lawrence was late in breaking up that spring; besides which, as soon as the snow began to thaw, the journey by road could become both unpleasant and dangerous.

"I must say that I shall be more than happy to put my feet on terra firma once more." Eliza sighed. "And I am already quite convinced that I will never again have the courage to make this trip, no matter what conditions are like in Canada."

Caroline refused to comment, but her aunt's words reminded her of D'Arcy Letton's wager. No matter how adverse the conditions, she was bound to stay there for at least a year from the time they arrived; and there had already been many occasions when she had begun to have vague doubts about her ability to endure the coarse life for that length of time. She soon dismissed her fears, however, for they had not yet arrived at their destination. Undoubtedly things would be much better in Upper Canada, or her uncle would not have remained there all these years.

Eliza Fairchild looked at her niece anxiously and inquired if she was feeling quite well, for rumour had reached them that fever had broken out amongst some of the steerage passengers.

"Oh, no, I'm really feeling quite indelicately healthy," Caroline reassured her. "But," she continued with a look of vague concern, "I was witness to a most unpleasant incident and I had reason to call young Mr. Paine's attention to it. A young boy who had brought his bucket for the daily fresh-water ration was told by the great bully of a sailor who was ladling it out that it had all gone for that day. When the lad protested, the wretched man beat him about the head with an iron bar, and I fear the child was badly cut about."

Hannah, a plump motherly little woman, pursed her lips in disapproval. "I can well believe that, my lady. You should see the conditions under which they have to live. Why, the animals on your uncle's farm are better provided for than those poor souls, and some of the crew treat them like cattle or slaves. But don't trouble your head, ma'am; I'll make it my business to go and take a look at the boy."

"Yes, please do," Eliza was quick to reply. "And take some of the unguent we brought with us."

They were both greatly relieved when Hannah reported

back to them later that day that young Patrick Ryan, for that was the lad's name, was as well as could be expected. She said his mother had been most grateful for the ointment and had told her that they, too, were bound for Upper Canada. Mrs. Ryan had said that if they were fortunate enough to obtain a reasonable passage from New York, she would like to call upon them in York Town and thank the ladies personally.

Stephen Fairchild had arranged with some friends in New York to arrange the final stage of their journey. And after spending a few days in that bustling city to recover from their long sea voyage, the two ladies, accompanied by Hannah, set out to complete their trip to Upper Canada. They travelled by the Hudson and Mohawk rivers, arriving finally at Oswego on the American shore of Lake Ontario. From thence a small schooner took them on the last leg of their journey across the lake.

Their experiences throughout the entire journey had given Caroline some idea of the many difficulties of travelling in the New World; there had often been times when she had longed to be back in the safety and comfort of London. Many of the things she had witnessed had shocked her profoundly, and she had to confess that much of what D'Arcy had said regarding the behaviour of the people and their lack of manners proved to be only too true. They showed little respect for law and order, and none at all for rank. But as her aunt had said, when trying to console her, you could hardly expect anything else from the people in the States. They were, after all, for the most part renegade Englishmen who had but recently rebelled against their own sovereign. She was sure that they would find York the epitome of culture and civilization, and they would feel much more at home.

Caroline was standing on deck gazing across at the Canadian shore of the lake when her reverie was rudely interrupted by the sound of a gun echoing across the water. It startled her so that she nearly jumped out of her skin. One of the crew who was busy nearby laughed at her consternation.

"'Tis naught but the noon gun from the garrison over yonder." He pointed toward a collection of low buildings on a rise near the shore to the west of the harbour. "And that there with the lighthouse be Gibraltar Point."

The schooner was just rounding a point on the long sandy peninsula that guarded the harbour, and Caroline was able to distinguish a small white cottage set amidst the pines and poplars at the foot of the lighthouse and a flagstaff with the Union Jack.

"See the Jack?" her guide went on. "That's to let the folk know there be a vessel coming from the east. Were we coming from the other way, it'd be the red ensign, see!"

Caroline smiled and moved away. She was pleased to have the information, but she couldn't accustom herself to the familiar manner in which the common people addressed their betters. But for the moment she had other things to command her attention. As she looked across the green sward that topped the low cliffs bordering the shoreline, there was a line of trees, their branches still bare of leaf, but from the line and size, she imagined them to be oaks. Beyond them was a low wooden building which she took to be a stable, but they were still too far for her to make out any detail. Her eye travelled across the small clearing that was the capital of Upper Canada to the dense forests that ringed it on all three sides, stretching as far as the eye could see. Her emotions were a strange mixture of awe and fear as they drew nearer. She had already seen enough of the New World to know that much of it still was virgin forest, but she was ill-prepared for such a wilderness. There was a compelling majesty about the tall dark pines, their tops still white with winter snow, silent and foreboding against the clear azure of an April sky.

As the small schooner drew closer to a wooden jetty with a large building sporting the sign "Cooper's Wharf," her aunt and Hannah joined her up on deck. They too were anxious to see the capital city of their new home. For some time they had been hearing the sound of a tin horn heralding their arrival, and the wharf was already a hive of activity.

On a curve of beach leading toward the peninsula, there was a wigwam, and Caroline was able to distinguish a group of Indians sorting fish. They stood upright as the ship approached and gazed at it solemnly with their dark eyes. Several rugged-looking men waded through the flags and rushes to adjust the mooring ropes along the jetty. Over the heads of the crowd the ladies could see a muddy track, for one could hardly call it a road, leading up toward the town. It was lined with a motley assortment of vehicles; smart carriages rubbed wheels with wagons of all descriptions; some were horse-drawn, but many had oxen between their shafts. Their occupants were already waiting on the wharf to meet passengers like themselves or take receipt of the goods with which the ship was loaded.

Caroline, determined to make a good impression on her arrival, had put on her new fawn velvet pelisse over a muslin gown, and wore a high-crowned poke bonnet trimmed with flowers. The sharp breeze from the lake had brought the colour to her cheeks and, as her aunt had told her, she looked as radiant as a spring day. However, as she viewed the track beyond the wharf, her spirits were somewhat dampened, for it was awash with thick mud. It squelched underfoot as the bystanders hurried forward, assailing them with cries of greeting. Not even the ladies appeared in the least worried that in some places it was well over the ankles, for they had come prepared and were wearing wooden pattens or heavy woollen socks over their light shoes.

As soon as the gangplank was in place, the Honourable Stephen Fairchild was the first person aboard. A small rotund man in his late fifties, he doffed his tall hat and welcomed them both warmly. Having kissed and hugged his sister with a complete lack of self-consciousness and disregard for decorum, he did the same to Caroline, to the infinite joy of a number of the onlookers, who called out asking if they might join him.

"Why, my dear, what a remarkably handsome young lady you have become. You were scarcely more than a babe when last I saw you. I can see that you will set many hearts aflutter amongst the young bucks in our society." Caroline blushed prettily, but it was impossible to be put out by his blunt manner, for it was plain to see his affection was sincere.

Suddenly he noticed Hannah standing a short distance behind them, and hurried forward to grasp her hand. "Why, if it isn't my old friend Hannah Tippet," he said warmly. For a moment Caroline thought that Miss Fairchild was going to have apoplexy, and she was thankful that no one of account was present to witness such uncalled-for familiarity toward a servant. But apart from raising their eyebrows at each other to mark their dismay, they chose to ignore Mr. Fairchild's conduct, putting it down to the infectious joy of the reunion.

Stephen quickly set about organizing the unloading of the few pieces of luggage they had brought with them. Their trunks and heavy baggage had been put aboard a bateau and would arrive later, as the craft was slower and took a longer route around the lake.

Having directed his man Henry to attend to it with Hannah, he said, "I have my carriage waiting, for although it is but a few steps to my house on King Street, I guessed that you might not be suitably dressed to deal with our spring thaw." He glanced appraisingly over the ladies' modish apparel. Then, taking his sister's arm, he guided her carefully down the gangplank, calling to Caroline to await his return.

As he reached the wharf, he was approached by a tall broad-shouldered young man whom Caroline supposed to be another of his servants. The fellow was wearing a full-sleeved coarse grey woollen shirt with thick flannel breeches, his boots scarcely visible under the thick coating of mud. But she noted that he had a pleasant enough face under a thick untidy mop of fair curly hair. She had seen him amongst the group of young men who had been joshing her uncle when he had first embraced her.

He exchanged some words with Mr. Fairchild, who turned and gestured toward Caroline, and she supposed he was giving the man orders with regard to the baggage. However, she was far from ready for what happened next. With a few easy strides he was soon aboard and smiling down at her.

"Good morning, ma'am. Your uncle has asked me to see you reach his carriage safely. He's somewhat concerned, as he feels you are not suitably attired to cope with 'Muddy York'—and I can well see why." His merry eyes had been taking in every detail of Caroline's elegant appearance.

"Thank you," she said stiffly, feeling that his manner was a mite too familiar for his position, although she was surprised by his speech, which had the polish acquired only by a good education and breeding.

"I'm afraid there is only one way I can think of that will prevent you spoiling those pretty clothes of yours." And without further ado he swept her up into his arms as though she were a piece of thistledown. By the time Caroline had recovered from her surprise, she was too firmly encircled in his iron grasp to attempt to struggle.

A gale of laughter went up from the group on shore, and several of them hurried to the edge of the wharf and invited him to toss her over and they would catch her. He looked down at her mischievously. "That really would be quite a notable way for you to arrive amongst us, ma'am!" he said in the slightly unfamiliar accent that she was beginning to associate with North Americans.

She felt the arms holding her against his broad chest relax slightly, and for one awful moment Caroline was afraid he was going to comply with their suggestion. "Don't you dare," she cried. "I'll have your master whip you if you try such a thing."

Her captor laughed gaily at the suggestion. "I doubt that very much, ma'am. He's far too fond of me to do anything so barbaric. But have no fear, I'm enjoying my task far too much to share it with any other man."

Caroline was in no position to stand upon her dignity. She could only lower her eyes as he stared down at her with an expression of admiration tinged with amusement. In spite of her added weight, his movements were swift and easy, and they were soon beside the waiting carriage. He lowered her gently into it and stooped to make sure her skirts cleared the door before closing it. At least he had some of the manners of a gentleman.

"Thank you! I am much obliged," she said, hoping he would go away and save her from any further embarrassment. But he turned to Mr. Fairchild with a broad grin.

"And now, sir, I think that you owe it to me to introduce us, for I fear your niece feels her fine feathers have been ruffled by an uncouth fellow who deserves a good whipping!"

"Good heavens," her uncle exclaimed. "We must correct that impression at once. You must excuse my lack of courtesy, but the excitement of seeing some of my family again has quite eclipsed anything else." He turned first to his sister. "Eliza, my dear, may I present Captain Pierce Chinery . . . and this is my niece, Lady Caroline Fairchild." Then, noticing her utter confusion, he hastened to add, "Pierce is one of the most promising young men in our little community, and a dear friend of mine, so you will have plenty of opportunity to get better acquainted. He really is a most splendid fellow."

Captain Chinery stood smartly to attention and gave a slight bow. "My pleasure and your servant ladies! And I hope that Lady Caroline will be prepared to overlook the rude manners of a rough colonial. Next time we meet, I will do my best to make amends for any embarrassment I may have caused her. Now, if you will excuse me, I have to go and attend to the unloading of some building materials I have ordered. I am sincerely hoping they have brought the glass for my windows, for it has been an unconscionably cold winter, with only greased paper to keep out the snow." He gave another bow and strode swiftly back toward the dockside, where a number of crates had been deposited.

Caroline was too abashed to look up. But her aunt said, "Good heavens, surely Captain Chinery doesn't have to attend to such menial tasks himself. Has he no staff?"

Stephen Fairchild gave a dry little laugh. "Oh, my dear Eliza, I'm afraid you have some rude shocks in store for you, although I did my best to warn you. I said that servants were hard to come by over here. Even the wealthiest amongst us can number no more than four or five in their household. I am most fortunate at the moment, for I have a cook who acts as my housekeeper, and a maid as well as Henry, here." He indicated the elderly man who had been assisting Hannah and was now piling their luggage onto the wagon drawn up behind them.

"Great Jehoshaphat!" Eliza exclaimed. "Why, we have more than five and twenty in London alone, and heaven knows how many in the country. Are they so lazy that they won't work for good wages?"

"Oh, no," her brother hastened to assure her. "Laziness is not one of the common faults amongst the good people in these parts. If it were, not many would survive. But there are fewer than a thousand of us in York and its environs, and every settler is soon able to buy a parcel of land which he can call his own. Why should any man wish to work for another when he can be his own master? The only alternative would be to follow the States, but Canada has never condoned slavery, although, unfortunately, we still have some who favour it. But most of the black people you see here are free. Those who remain in bondage are the older ones who came here as slaves with their masters after the revolution. Hopefully there will soon be no more of them, if the law has its way."

"I should hope so," his sister was prompt to reply, for she was a staunch supporter of Mr. Wilberforce.

Her uncle's words regarding a man's personal liberty caused Caroline some consternation. There were, of course, no slaves in England, but a servant was subject to his master's authority, and whipping was still a common form of discipline. She recalled the way she had rebuked Captain Chinery. No wonder he had laughed at the thought of taking a whip to himself and found the mere idea barbaric.

Henry, with Hannah up beside him, was driving the wagon, so Mr. Fairchild took the ribbons of their carriage himself. It was with a mighty effort that the horses managed to pull them out of the mud, but slowly they started their journey toward the town.

Their route took them past the church of St. James, a plain wooden structure placed some yards back from the road. Stephen Fairchild spoke of it with pride, having been one of the prime movers in getting it built. But comparing it to the Abbey or St. Paul's Cathedral back home, Caroline was not impressed. It was a mere fifty feet long, with gables at either end and a double row of windows on either side. A few pine trees and a snake fence were the only other things that decorated the lot.

The carriage rattled over a plank bridge spanning one of the many rivulets that flowed through York and past the wooden stockade that surrounded the jail. They continued on over Yonge Street, which their host explained would soon be cleared through to the north and allow a much faster route for the fur traders and farmers bringing their goods to the lake for shipment. Caroline was growing more and more despondent throughout the guided tour. Her thoughts turned to Bond Street with its elegant shops, the gardens at Vauxhall, and riding in Rotten Row on a sunny April morning. Her uncle reined in the horses and waited for Henry to open a handsome pair of ornamental iron gates. They looked a little incongruous set in a fence of short wooden palings on a low stone wall.

Miss Fairchild lifted her quizzing glass and stared at a sign over an apothecary's shop a few yards down the road. "Is it the custom over here to allow tradespeople to conduct their business in a residential area, Stephen?" She was not a snob, but she had never recovered from the censure of the family when they had found that she had inadvertently sat next to the wife of a wealthy grocer at an assembly.

"You have to remember, Eliza, that little more than twenty years ago this entire area was virgin forest. The settlers at that time could not afford to consider the niceties of such social distinctions. In most cases here you will find that the residence is also their place of business. In my own case, I have my office in my house, which is one of the reasons we are so cramped."

"But you are a government official," Eliza retorted, a note of pained surprise in her voice. "I should have thought they would have provided you with suitable accommodation according to your rank."

"You forget two years ago the Yankees burned down our government buildings. But even so, it is the habit to conduct one's business from the place of residence."

Caroline made no comment; she was too busy wondering where the *haut ton* of York could possibly reside, for as yet she hadn't seen a house fit for a lady or gentleman to live in. They certainly could not be compared with Walford House or any of the mansions she was used to frequenting.

The Fairchild house was a low two-storey square log structure, part of which had been covered with white-painted clapboard. It had a handsome doorway with a glass transom over it and wide wooden steps leading up to the veranda that ran along the front.

"I started to make some improvements while Agnes was alive, as she did not wish to leave this house, having come to it as a bride," Stephen said. "But it has always been my desire to acquire one of the larger lots on Front Street, especially now my family is growing."

As he mentioned his family, the front door was thrown open and a group of laughing children tumbled out of it to greet them. Stephen quickly introduced them as his two sons—Joseph, a quiet studious lad of fourteen, and Mark, a mischievous ten-year-old—and his daughter, Priscilla, a pretty little girl of six who took to Caroline immediately. Behind them stood a sour-faced woman with an infant of about a year in her arms. It was plain to see that she did not share in the general excitement of their arrival.

"This is Agnes Hepple, my housekeeper," Stephen said, taking the baby from her. "And this is little Ben, whose birth, as you know, was unfortunately the cause of my poor wife's demise. But he's a fine boy, don't you think, Eliza?" Quite unceremoniously he dumped the child into his sister's arms, taking the poor lady completely by surprise. "Keep an eye on him while Agnes makes us some tea. The boys and I will attend to your luggage. Henry has to take care of the horses. And, Prissy, you take your cousin up to the guest bedroom."

For the next half-hour the whole house was a scurry of activity, everyone having a task to perform. Caroline was at a loss to know what she should do until she felt a small hand slipped into hers. Little Prissy looked up into her face and said in a quaint grown-up way, "If you come with me, Cousin Caroline, I will show you to your room."

Obediently Caroline followed her small cousin up the bare wooden staircase that led from the front hall. On the white plastered walls there were several family portraits that her uncle had obviously brought with him from England, as he had also done much of the beautiful furniture in the front parlour, together with a fine Turkey carpet, which was the family's pride and joy. The walls in there had been covered with a handsome paper imported from the States, but upstairs, only the master bedroom sported paper, and the wooden floors were bare except for a scattering of multicolored rag rugs.

"You see, we have to wait until somebody goes back to England and sells their furniture off at the auction before we can get any more good furniture," Prissy explained apologetically, showing Caroline into a moderate-sized bedroom at the back of the house. "This is just some stuff Papa had made by Mr. Jenks." She waved a small hand toward a large bed with four rounded pillars at each corner and covered by a gaily coloured patchwork quilt. "I helped Agnes sort out the pieces for that," she added proudly.

The simple pieces were made of maple or cherry, highly polished, and smelling strongly of beeswax. Caroline ran her hands over the smooth surfaces, warm and solid beneath her touch. It was all so different from the fragile furniture and dainty silks and satins of her own palatial apartment at Walford House.

"Aunt Eliza will be sharing this room with you, but as you can see, there is plenty of room in the closets." Prissy struggled to reach the metal latch, and Caroline hurried forward to assist her.

"Thank you," the little girl said solemnly. "I'm doing my best to grow as quickly as I can so that I can take my turn in the house, but I'm not quite tall enough for some of the jobs yet."

Caroline smiled as she thought of the children of her friends back home. Most of them were grossly spoiled, having at least one servant of their own to attend to their needs. They would have been at a total loss to have played the hostess with like efficiency.

Prissy was on tiptoe, pulling the blue-and-white water pitcher in the bowl on the three-cornered washstand. "I thought he wouldn't," she said knowingly. "Agnes told Mark to fill this from the pump in the yard, but he tries to get out of doing his tasks whenever he can."

"Never mind," Caroline said, sitting down on the wooden blanket box at the end of the bed. "I expect he will get round to doing it as soon as he can. If not, I'll see to it. He's busy bringing in our luggage at the moment."

"I'll go and see if he's finished and tell him you're waiting for it," the child said gravely.

After she'd gone, Caroline took off her bonnet and pelisse and put them away in the large closet. It was already apparent that she could not expect the services of a personal maid to wait upon her. Thank heaven that Hannah had agreed to come with them. At least she'd be able to dress their hair and care for their wardrobe. She wandered across to the window and looked down onto the yard, where Henry was busy stabling the horses. There was the pump from which she had so glibly said she would fill her own pitcher, but never in her life had she been called upon to do such a thing, and she had grave doubts as to whether she could make it work. No doubt little Prissy would be able to educate her.

Caroline was both shocked and amused by the circumstances in which she found herself. Then she was suddenly overwhelmed by a great feeling of homesickness. She felt so alone in this alien land whose customs were strange to her. The only comfort she could find was the thought that she was unlikely to be bored, especially if the rest of the young men in the town measured up to Captain Chinery.

Beyond the bleak muddy yard the trees were still bare of leaf, and there were no flowers to be seen; she contrasted it with the leafy hedges and abundant blossoms that would by now be filling the London squares. But the memory of the young captain kept intruding upon her thoughts. His manner had been truly audacious, yet she could not be mortally offended, for he had so plainly meant well. What a pity he was a colonial, for he was far more attractive than any of the young bucks who graced her uncle's drawing room in London. And she had no doubt from the feel of his strong arms that he could have held his own with the lot of them at any of their favourite sports.

His mode of dress was quite outlandish, and no doubt he lacked the necessary social graces to make him acceptable to the *haut ton*. Yet, Caroline had to confess, when they were officially introduced, he had acted with perfect decorum. It was silly on such a short acquaintance, but she found her heart fluttering at the thought of meeting him again.

She did not have long to wait. Over supper that evening Mr. Fairchild told them that they were to be the guests of honour at an assembly the following night. Apparently the arrival of a duke's daughter, having both a title and a fortune in her own right, had set their little circle in quite a twitter. Everyone was competing to be the first to entertain Caroline and her aunt, but the commanding officer of the garrison had beaten them all to it.

"It's just as well," Stephen remarked. "For you have no idea how quick to take offense some of our good ladies seem to be. We had a most unfortunate affair some years back, when one of their number considered she had been slighted and forced her husband into a duel that led to his untimely death. I'm afraid that you will find that precedence is quite as important here as it is at home, at least amongst our twenty best families. Of course things are changing rapidly, and a great number of the younger people refuse to be bound by it. And I really can't say I blame them; Pierce Chinery is a case in point."

Eliza Fairchild raised her eyebrows. "Do you mean by that he is not acceptable? He seemed a remarkably pleasant young man."

"Well, let us just say that he is on the borderline. He is in the unfortunate position of being an American by birth. His family immigrated to New England some years before the revolution, but I understand they came from quite a good British bloodline. However, his people did not choose to espouse the Empire loyalist cause, and although he has now chosen to settle amongst us, his loyalty and social status are somewhat suspect in some quarters. This is compensated for by the fact that he appears to be quite well endowed financially."

"But you do not share that opinion of him, Uncle Stephen?" Caroline interrupted anxiously.

"Not at all," her uncle reassured her. "I find him a highly responsible and intelligent young fellow. Unlike many members of our so-called aristocracy over here, he had an excellent education, graduating from Harvard before doing a brief stint in the army. But anyone who attempts to alter the status quo these days is immediately labelled a Jacobin. Personally, I enjoy his company. He often joins me in the evening for a game of chess. And he's very popular amongst many members of the younger set, although several of the mamas seem to frown on him."

Caroline was eager to find out all she could about Captain Chinery before meeting him again. She told herself that it was important to know whether she could accept him into her circle of acquaintances, but her deeper feelings were telling her she would be unable to keep him out.

"What are his intentions now that he has given up the army?" She hoped her tone was one of casual interest. But her aunt, knowing her, looked across and smiled.

"He has recently purchased several acres near Spadina ridge, the old Indian trail that runs from the lake up north. He lives in a small log cabin but is building himself a house, and from what he tells me, it is well advanced. When I was last up there, it appeared that it will be a remarkably handsome property when it is finished."

"Then no doubt he will be bringing his wife to live in it?" Eliza said, anticipating her niece's line of inquiry.

"Oh, Pierce isn't married yet. Though I've no doubt it is on his mind. It is not easy for anyone to manage on their own out here, as you can see." Stephen leaned across and patted his sister's hand. "That is why I am only too grateful that you have come, my dear Eliza. It has been with great difficulty and a considerable sum of money that I have been able to persuade Agnes to stay with me until your arrival. She will be leaving us at the end of the month, I'm afraid. She is marrying a settler and going up into the bush to help him clear his land."

"I should have thought that she was past the marrying age," Eliza said.

"Out here we are not so inclined to put our womenfolk on the shelf as soon as they are past one-and-twenty. They play a much more positive part in our society, and the men cannot afford to choose them only for their beauty, much as they might like to," her brother replied.

The two ladies looked across the table at each other, an expression of consternation on their faces. They had already discussed the problems involved with the severe shortage of servants, and with Agnes gone there would be no one to do the cooking.

Eliza remarked on this, and Stephen replied, "I was hoping that Hannah might be willing to oblige. As I remember, she is a most competent person in all facets of housekeeping. With you two ladies to assist her, I feel sure that we can manage admirably. Mary, our little maid, is a willing child and can do most of the cleaning, but with a household of our size, I'm afraid it will mean that everyone has to do his share."

"I will speak to Hannah," Eliza said. "She has, of course, done everything in her time, but she has risen to the rank of my personal maid. However, she is not the kind to stand upon ceremony. As for us, I'm sure we shall settle into it all in time, and I shall be most happy to take the children off your hands. But it must be possible to obtain further assistance . . . perhaps if we were to offer them more money?"

Her brother sighed. "I'm afraid money is not all that important to many of them, once they have bought their land. You will discover that the old-fashioned method of barter still plays an important part in our financial dealings out here. The settlers bring in their corn and other crops and exchange it for the goods they need. The storekeepers send the crops to Lower Canada in exchange for other goods and so the round continues. Coins in themselves have little value—in fact, we use the currency of several nations. Out here, food, household goods, and clothing are of much more use."

"We shall have to start bartering off our wardrobes, that's all there is to it." Eliza laughed. "It's a good job we came provided in that area."

Caroline kept quiet. She was not prepared to exchange exquisite London and Paris fashions for a bushel of wheat. In fact, she felt she would rather starve first.

The Honourable Stephen Fairchild was one of the chief aides to his excellency the lieutenant governor, Sir Francis Gore, and as a scion of a most distinguished Bristish family, he was considered one of the leaders in the small elite group that ruled Upper Canada. Not only that, his two sons attended Dr. Strachan's highly exclusive school. Consequently, the morning after their arrival, Miss Fairchild and her niece were overcome by the number of people arriving to pay their respects and take the measure of the two newcomers to their set. At home it would have been up to them to let it be known when they were ready to receive, but over here it appeared things were done differently. And scarcely any of the visitors observed the niceties, failing to take their leave after the customary ten minutes—fifteen at the outside.

It was extremely difficult in a parlour full of chattering women for either Caroline or her aunt to distinguish one from the other, but two of their number made a deep impression: Mrs. John Kendall and her daughter Blanche. They did not waste a second before announcing to the assembled company that they had a prior claim on the Fairchilds' attention, as John Kendall's cousin Sir D'Arcy Letton was a particular friend of Lady Caroline's.

Caroline was relieved to find that apparently D'Arcy had made no mention of the wager in his communication with the Kendalls, but in any event she was not much taken with either of them and was pleased that the numbers present made it unnecessary for her to do more than exchange the usual pleasantries. When they departed, they did so with avowals that she must join their party at the assembly that evening, an invitation that Caroline silently rejected on the spot. After they had all gone, she asked her aunt for her opinions.

"I think, my dear, that your Uncle Stephen was quite correct when he said that several of the ladies were somewhat prickly over the right of precedence. I fear that we have all the failings of London society squeezed into a mighty small jar, and we shall have to be extremely careful not to do anything to make the top blow off."

Caroline gave a slight snort and tossed her head. "Well, I for one shall make my own rules. I fully intend to become acquainted with whomsoever I please."

"Of course, my dear, just so long as it doesn't harm your uncle's position in the community. But I wouldn't worry yet. From what I heard this morning, Captain Chinery has quite as many friends as enemies."

Caroline turned an overly innocent gaze on her aunt. "Whatever gave you the impression that I was thinking of him?"

"Because I've known you for so long, my dear niece. I can already recognize the Pierce Chinery look in your eyes. And since our arrival yesterday, you have been thinking of little else."

Caroline knew it was useless to contradict her aunt. She contented herself with saying, "If you are correct, then it is only because he is the one gentleman of my own age group that I have met so far."

"Of course," Eliza replied with irritating smoothness. "But I've no doubt that will be rectified this evening, for I'm sure you will be quite the belle of the ball. What are you going to wear—your new white gown with the pale blue sash?"

3

There was a brisk breeze blowing off the lake as they drove out of town along the tree-lined road leading to the garrison. And the stars glistened like a myriad diamonds in the clear deep blue of the April night. Once again Caroline was struck by the awesome majesty of their surroundings. It was so very different from the gentle rolling countryside in which she had grown up. It was both fascinating and fearsome, with the great forests stretching away into the distance, hiding heaven alone knew what unexpected dangers. Her uncle had told them that the Indians were quite friendly, and it was rarely that they saw any wild beasts in the streets of the town. But Caroline found little comfort in that. Out there, in the darkness, she sensed there were all kinds of living things, and each one could prove a potential danger.

Her Aunt Eliza gave voice to her fears: "It is comforting to feel such a solid coach around us, for I would feel uncommonly exposed on horseback under such conditions."

"You'll soon get used to it, my dear," her brother replied. "But I'm pleased to know you like the coach. I only took delivery of it last week, and I'm particularly proud of it, as it was made locally. Before very long, Montreal and some of the cities in the States will have to look to their laurels, for we are rapidly becoming quite industrialized." He peered out into the darkness and then said reassuringly, "But as you can see, we are not alone on the road. There are several other carriages ahead—far more than usual. Your visit is causing quite a flutter."

Stephen Fairchild leaned back and gave a slight smirk of pride. He was normally a gentle, unprepossessing little man. Without his family connections, he would never have had the mental stamina to reach his present position, so he was naturally pleased to think that for once his little party would be the centre of interest.

"You should both be doubly flattered that we have such

a turnout. There is to be an election for a member of the legislative assembly in a few weeks' time, and normally the gentlemen would have been far too busy to attend."

"Buying votes for their candidate, as they do in England, no doubt?" Caroline remarked caustically.

"My dear niece"—Stephen was gently reproving—"it is just politic to do so. After all, we have to make sure that the right people are in a position to wield power. We can't allow any Tom, Dick, or Harry to be elected."

"But if you don't let some of the ordinary people have a say in how the country should be run, they will behave like those wretched traitors down in the States," his sister replied sharply. "Though I think they went much too far, I have a sneaking sympathy for them. Why should they pay taxes without adequate representation?"

Stephen fidgetted nervously with his lace cravat. He was a peace-loving man and he had a sudden uneasy feeling that the two female members of his family could prove more than he could handle. "I do beg you both to be discreet in your remarks regarding our political situation. We are not yet ready for the outspokenness you indulge in back home. There is an undercurrent of unrest about these days. Many people are apprehensive about the newcomers that are moving into the district, particularly the Americans. They think they may have come to encourage the settlers to revolt against the Executive."

"You say Pierce Chinery is one of them, yet you claim him as a friend," Caroline was swift to interrupt.

"Yes, because I like him and I don't think he's a radical to that extent. Although I must admit he is inclined to be outspoken on some issues, particularly with regard to the clergy reserves, and I have warned him to be cautious."

"From what I have seen, I do not imagine caution to be one of Captain Chinery's traits." Caroline smiled as she remembered the authoritative way he had taken command of her the previous day. "He strikes me as being the kind of man who acts first and asks permission later. But I suppose you can expect little else from a wild backwoodsman."

"He is one of the few with the education and leadership qualities that pose a threat to the small clique in power. He may not have the polish of your London bucks, for admittedly he pays little heed to his appearance, but don't dismiss him as an ignoramus. However, don't worry your pretty head about politics. Leave that for the gentlemen; ladies will never be able to understand all the intricacies involved in governing a country, especially a wild one like this. Politics aside, we have a most congenial little group here in York Town."

They had turned in through the gates of the stone walls with their wooden palisades that surrounded the fort. The sentries in their red jackets, grey trousers, and tall shakos came smartly to attention as they recognized the coat of arms on the door of the coach. Passing the log-built blockhouse, they came to a stop outside a new single-storey brick building, which Stephen told them was the recently completed officers' mess. Most of the old buildings had been destroyed by the Americans during the recent war.

Through the white-painted square-paned windows Caroline could see that an elegant company had already assembled. The strains of a small regimental band wafted through the wide doorway. And there was a general air of jollity, which boded well for a happy evening.

The ladies were shown into a small withdrawing room set aside for their use when the officers and gentlemen retired to the smoking room to play cards. It was pleasantly furnished, with a small spinet in one corner and a bright fire burning in the hearth. This evening it was being used as a powder room, and one of the soldier's wives was there to act as ladies' maid.

Caroline sat behind the small slipper screen while the woman stooped to change her shoes. This time she had been careful to heed her uncle's warning and had brought her dainty satin slippers with her. But she had noticed that the flag path outside the mess had been quite free of mud, the fort being well up on high ground.

Her Aunt Eliza, looking quite beautiful in an apple-green taffeta gown, was almost as excited as a young girl attending her first ball. "You know, Caroline, I feel absurdly young and unencumbered by my age quite suddenly. It's really most ridiculous, and as Stephen reminded me, I must behave with decorum."

Caroline patted a few of her bronze curls into place and joined her aunt by the door. "You are never anything but decorous, my dear aunt. I'm the rebel in the camp, and I have absolutely no intention of changing my ways. I fully intend to choose my friends from whomsoever I please."

"You always have, my dear." Her aunt laughed. "But let us hope there will be no more D'Arcy Lettons for you to wager with."

"Don't worry," Caroline replied gaily. "I have only one hand to give in marriage, and that is impounded for a year at least."

The announcement of their arrival caused quite a flurry. General Drewitt, the commander of the garrison, presented his lady and then his officers and the wives of the few that were married. Most of the other ladies, Caroline had already met that morning, but they were eager to present their husbands and sons.

The young men, of course, were only too anxious to pay their respects, for Caroline was looking radiant. She was wearing her white satin high-waisted gown with its overslip of silk gauze, long white kid gloves—and Hannah had dressed her hair in a small topknot of curls.

"May I have the pleasure of the first dance, Lady Caroline?" a thickset young man asked, anxious to exclude the others pressing around her with their cards.

"No, you may not, Chad," a quiet voice from behind her drawled. "This lady is already in my debt, and I demand payment for services rendered."

Caroline turned around swiftly and found herself gazing up into the laughing grey eyes of Pierce Chinery. But if it hadn't been for his lean, strong face, she might well have been at a loss to recognize him. There was no trace of the uncouth colonial in his appearance tonight. He was dressed in the very height of fashion—high-collared blue velvet coat and pale nankeen trousers, the soft frills of his silk shirt cascading over a satin waistcoat. The unruly curls had been tamed, and he presented a most elegant picture that quite took her breath away. Not waiting for her answer, he swept her onto the floor amidst the good-tempered protests of the others.

"Don't you ever wait for a lady to give you her answer, Captain Chinery?" Caroline rebuked him mildly.

"Not when I know what the answer will be," he said, guiding her smoothly over the polished floor. He was a most skilled dancer, and Caroline was aware that they made a handsome couple.

"Nonetheless, it would be a courtesy, for a lady has the right to make up her own mind."

"Sometimes." He laughed down at her. "But not when it crosses my wishes. You see, ma'am, I am only a part-time gentleman. At other times I mingle with the savages. And like all wild creatures, my behaviour can be unpredictable."

"Then I shall have to be on my guard and make sure

that I am always well armed," she said, blushing beneath the frank admiration of his gaze.

"Oh, you are more than well endowed with weapons, ma'am. But unfortunately, they do not serve as a protection, they tend rather to aggravate a man's desires."

"You are exceedingly outspoken, considering this is only our second meeting, Captain Chinery." Caroline mumbled the words against the soft silk on his chest.

"Possibly, ma'am. But in this country a man soon learns that he must go after what he wants. If I had not been bold, I would have been standing back there with the rest of the pack begging for your favour."

"And you are not a man to beg, Captain Chinery?" Caroline raised her eyes and found that the grey ones staring down at her were now quite serious in their intent. "Nor, I imagine, would you be willing to wager?"

"Only on a horse, ma'am. If it's anything I really want, then I make it my policy to just get up and go for it, with no messin', as we say in these parts. But I guess that wouldn't go down too well in the fancy society you're accustomed to."

Caroline felt that Captain Chinery's tone was slightly derisive, and she showed her annoyance. "It is unlikely that you are in a position to judge what we might do when we are put to a fence, sir."

"Now come, ma'am, there's no need for you to get all stiff and hoity-toity with me. I meant no offense. But when I was in London last, I went to one of your large assemblies with a friend of mine. And I just stood around watching some of those young bucks a-quizzing the young ladies and bowing and scraping to each other. Giving way all the time, when you could just tell they were itching to get the gal."

"Really, Captain Chinery," Caroline said icily. "And you could tell all that from just watching them? How do you know they didn't get the one they wanted in the end? We no longer consider it necessary to settle disputes by brute force. We leave that kind of behaviour to the farm dogs." Fortunately the music came to an end at that moment and Caroline was immediately swept into the next dance by Chad Kendall.

She had to make a determined effort to compose herself and not allow her partner to see that Pierce Chinery had ruffled her feathers. Chad was an amiable young gentleman but far from bright, so it was not hard to keep up a conversation with him.

Pierce Chinery had gone over and was talking to a small,

dark little girl who had been standing in the corner and looked very much alone. Whenever he looked in her direction, which happened quite frequently, Caroline made a point of laughing gaily at whatever fatuous remark Chad happened to be making. After they had passed them on one occasion, Caroline asked about the girl.

"I don't think I had the pleasure of making her acquaintance when the ladies came to call this morning," she remarked.

"Oh, that is Miss Anna Thomas. She's the niece of the old gentleman talking to Miss Fairchild. He's the Count de la Fayre."

"A French-Canadian?" Caroline queried.

"No, he's one of several royalists that settled here after their revolution. My ma . . . mama says," he corrected himself quickly, "they used to be of some importance, but now they lost all their money; they ain't no better than the rest of the settlers. Have you ever been to Paris, France, Lady Fairchild?" Poor Chad tried valiantly to keep up the tone of the conversation. "I ain't never been further than Montreal myself, except of course for the time we spent in Halifax, but then I weren't nothing but a boy, so it don't . . . doesn't count, I guess."

Caroline refrained from telling him that she had been to most of the European countries of any account. She felt it would be too much for the young man to contend with. He was plainly feeling uncomfortable, and this was made worse by the unspoken signals he kept receiving from Mrs. Kendall, who hardly took her eyes off them. She was obviously pleased that her son had obeyed orders and managed to be one of the first to dance with Lady Caroline, who was heartily pleased when the music finished.

Chad passed her on to a tall, handsome man whom he introduced as Colonel Oliver Rowlands and who was a far more accomplished dancer. "I expect you find this very provincial after London society, Lady Caroline? Heaven knows, I do. I sometimes think I must have been completely out of my mind when I agreed to come here."

"You are not a native of these parts, then, Colonel?" Caroline said, looking up into his dark brooding eyes.

"God forbid! Do I look like a country yokel?"

Caroline was quick to admit that he looked far from it, for his clothes were of the latest fashion. In fact, for elegance of appearance he ran Pierce Chinery a very close second, and he was almost as handsome in a dark saturnine way.

"No, I sold my commission after Waterloo. I decided that it was time I settled down and looked about for a wife. Then my cousin offered me a remarkably good position in the government and a free land grant of several hundred acres. The offer was far too good to refuse."

"But you don't think that you will stay here?"

"For the rest of my days? The mere thought of it appalls me, Lady Caroline. I intend to wrest every penny I can from this godforsaken hole and then hightail it back to civilization as soon as possible. I take it that you are merely paying a courtesy visit to your uncle, for I cannot imagine anyone of your quality finding it congenial for more than a month or two."

In spite of his cool sophisticated manner, there was something about Oliver Rowlands that jarred on Caroline's sensibilities. She came to the conclusion that he reminded her too much of D'Arcy Letton, and she had no wish to think of *him* at the moment.

She was relieved to suddenly find that everyone was dancing and there was no young man in sight to claim her hand. Quickly she slipped outside, thankful to get some fresh air. She collected her large paisley shawl, and wrapping it around her shoulders against the keen night air, she walked out of the door and down the narrow flagged path. She stood for a moment looking out across the bay to where the lighthouse blinked its warning to passing ships.

Caroline turned and looked back at the dark forests that covered the hills on either side. On the far ridge, tall pines patterned the moon in filigree; away from the candlelight and the sound of the band playing, she again experienced a great sense of loneliness. But this time it was different; this time she was not homesick, it was as if she suddenly felt an urge to run into the great darkness yonder and meld with it, as though some magic power were drawing her toward the forest. She turned the corner of the long low building and started down the grassy bank, but she had not gone more than a step or two when an unearthly sound made her nearly jump out of her skin and her blood turn to ice. She stood frozen to the spot, unable to move as it came again and again, her panic mounting with each howl.

Just when Caroline thought her heart must burst with fear, she found herself wrapped in a pair of strong warm arms. "This is mighty foolish of you, ma'am," Pierce Chinery said in his soft drawl. "You could catch your death of cold on a night like this." He was wearing a heavy riding cloak, and he pulled it about them both, so that she stood with her head against his broad chest.

Caroline made no attempt to move, for she had never been so pleased to see anyone so much in all her life. "That noise . . . it curdled my blood."

Pierce gave a gentle laugh. "You don't need to be afeared of that, ma'am. It's only the wolves calling to each other—" He had been about to say they would not harm her, but at the mention of the word "wolves," Caroline had turned and clung to him. And as he was not at all averse to their situation, he said no more. But drawing her still closer against his body, he kissed her passionately upon the lips. Not once or twice, but several times before Caroline was able to regain her breath.

"Captain Chinery!" she finally managed to gasp, scandalized by his behaviour. "Please unhand me this minute," but she made no attempt to struggle.

"Pierce," he said, his grey eyes gazing serenely down into her amber ones. "After that, I think you should call me Pierce, and I'll call you Caroline, or would you prefer Carrie?"

"Certainly not!" she exploded indignantly. "We are not on such familiar terms."

"Well, maybe you're not, Caroline, but I sure am. I reckon that makes us kind of kissing cousins from now on, don't you?"

"In my poisition, I am not used to being treated like that, whatever may be the custom out here."

His eyes glinted merrily—he was not in the least put off by her show of indignation. "Your position right at this moment, Caroline, is in my arms. And when I hold a beautiful young woman in my arms and she's not there for dancing with, then I reckon there's only one thing left to do." And suiting the action to the word, he once more pressed his warm firm mouth against hers, holding her so close against his hard lean body that she had no breath to protest.

Then, swinging her up into his arms as he had done the day before, he said, "Now I'll take you back, or your folks will be wondering what's become of you."

Caroline's head was whirling with any number of things she felt beholden to say. But all she could manage to splutter as he set her down by the door was: "A gentleman would never have dreamed of doing such a thing."

He raised her hand to his lips and said, "That's where you're wrong, ma'am. A gentleman would have dreamed of doing it, but only a man would have done it." Then, with a broad grin, he turned and strode off into the darkness, leaving Caroline to go back into the ballroom alone.

Eliza Fairchild had noticed her absence and had come looking for her. "Caroline, my dear child, where have you been? . . . And what has happened to you—you look as though you have seen a ghost."

"No, I'm quite all right. I went outside for a breath of air because I was feeling somewhat faint, and . . . and . . ." She suddenly found that she could not put into words what she had just experienced. Nor, she found to her amazement, did she particularly want to share it with anyone, not even her beloved aunt, just at the moment. Later of course she would tell her; and Pierce Chinery would have to be dealt with for his insolence. "I heard some wolves howling, and I was scared. Then Captain Chinery found me and brought me back here."

"How very fortunate," Eliza Fairchild said. "He really is a very nice young man. He came to pay his respects and say that he was leaving, as he has some distance to go, and he appeared so disappointed that you were not there with us. But your uncle has invited him to dinner tomorrow night, so I will be able to thank him then."

"Yes, aunt," her niece said meekly, and went into the powder room to tidy her hair before returning to the dance.

For the remainder of the evening's festivities Caroline did her best to appear congenial. But now that Pierce Chinery was no longer present, she quickly found it becoming a bore. Many of the young men, like Chad Kendall, were little more than country bumpkins, for all their wealth and position. Finding they and Caroline had little in common to talk about, and more often than not at a loss for words, they soon returned to their more familiar partners.

Caroline, much to her relief, was left with a small coterie of admirers, amongst the foremost of whom was Colonel Oliver Rowlands. He told her that he was building a large mansion on Front Street. "I should be much obliged, Lady Caroline, if you could spare the time to advise me over the furnishings. I have no doubt that your taste is impeccable, and you are of course *au courant* with all the latest fashions. I intend to import all the furniture, for I find this local stuff only fit for a peasant's cottage."

"The style is vastly different, I must admit. But some of the wood is quite beautiful," Caroline said, thinking of the lovely markings on her bed at Uncle Stephen's house.

After a time Colonel Rowlands' continually negative approach to everything Canadian became rather tedious. Caroline was well able to judge for herself that many of the customs were quaint and countrified. And although she had observed how touchy many of them were on the question of precedence, nevertheless the various ranks of society were not clearly defined or as carefully acknowledged as they would have been at one of the assemblies at Almack's. The behaviour of some of the young bloods would soon have given cause for them to be called out to answer for their discourtesy. This lack of finesse had been all too obvious in Pierce Chinery's behaviour.

While suffering the clumsy dancing of most of her partners and murmuring noncommittal answers to their questions, Caroline amused herself thinking of the various ways she might put Captain Chinery in his place. She had an uncomfortable feeling that it was going to prove a difficult task. For on the two occasions that he had behaved so presumptuously, he had also done her a service for which she had been grateful. Not only that, he had a merry way of looking at her, as though he knew quite well what she was thinking about his audacity and had every intention of continuing his wayward behaviour. He tended to remind her of the hound she had had in England; as a puppy it would pull at her skirts, and no amount of scolding would deter it from its purpose. Kissing cousins, indeed! But instead of being outraged, Caroline had the greatest difficulty not to laugh outright. Perhaps, after all, she should ignore it, for Pierce was a diverting companion and would help to pass away the time until she returned home.

During one of the intermissions her aunt introduced her to Count de la Fayre and his niece, Anna Thomas. He was not as old as she had first thought him, but was well into his fifties. He greeted her with Old World courtesy, but it was plain to see that it was Miss Eliza who had captured his attention.

Anna was a timid, pretty little girl a few years younger than Caroline, who had made note of the perfunctory way most of the other ladies present, especially Miss Kendall, had treated her. Consequently Caroline went out of her way to talk to her, and as soon as Anna found she was not going to be put in her place and talked down to, she became quite animated and the two girls found they had much in common. Before the evening was over, they had become quite good friends, much to the blatant disgust of Blanche Kendall.

"Of course, Lady Caroline," the latter remarked as the maid was changing their slippers prior to going home. "Far be it from me to tell you how to choose your companions. But as you are a newcomer in our midst, you cannot yet be acquainted with all the intricacies of our society." She smiled ingratiatingly at Caroline through watery grey eyes. She was a tall angular young woman with wispy straw-coloured hair, not a day under twenty-five. "Mutton dressed as lamb" had been Miss Fairchild's description of her after their first meeting.

"That's very true," Caroline replied rather acidly, aware that there was more to come. She had already made up her mind that Blanche was quite obnoxious, and moreover, she had seen the expression on Miss Kendall's face when Captain Chinery had claimed the first dance. Whether it was because the lady felt that her brother had been slighted or for some other reason, Caroline had yet to discover.

"Then may I suggest that you exercise some decorum with regard to Anna Thomas. She has no prospects and is not . . . how shall I say it . . . quite accepted by the best people in our set. Rather she is—"

"Merely tolerated," Caroline cut in abruptly. "I perfectly understand. We have many such people in England, although most of them, I'm happy to say, prefer to come to the colonies, where they can become big fish in a little pond rather than remaining such very small fish in a big one."

There was no mistaking the point of Caroline's remarks, and Blanche had the grace to blush. But Lady Caroline swept out of the room before Miss Kendall could think of a suitable reply.

"My dear, what did you say to upset Miss Kendall?" her aunt asked as they got into their carriage. "I quite thought she was going to explode."

Briefly Caroline told them of her conversation with the lady, adding how very enchanting she had found little Anna.

"It is a most unfortunate situation," Stephen Fairchild said. "The count, her uncle, is of course accepted because of his family. Although he is quite poor by the standards of most of the upper set out here. But his sister made the unforgivable *faux pas* of marrying a backwoodsman. I only saw the fellow once, but he seemed reasonably mannered. He had been a junior officer in the army and had the misfortune to be wounded . . . I remember he walked with a marked limp. . . . Anyway, he was given a small grant of land, and having little or no money, he had to do all the work himself. Anna's mother, in spite of being a lady by birth and upbringing, set to and helped him. As you can imagine, the ladies were horrified to see her doing such menial work. Then, shortly after Anna was born, the young couple came to an untimely death during an outbreak of cholera. Her uncle took the child to live with him, and now the two of them are devoted to each other, but Anna has never been considered quite acceptable, she is merely—"

"Tolerated," Caroline interrupted for the second time that evening. "Well, I for one like Anna, and I have absolutely no intention of bowing to their bourgeois prejudices."

"Hear! Hear!" her aunt agreed.

Stephen threw up his hands in mock despair. "Oh, dear! I can see that we are going to have quite a shake-up now that you two ladies have arrived. And although I must confess I tend to sit on the fence in such situations, for the simple reason that it can be very lonely if you cross the boundaries set by our small community, for once I am entirely in agreement with you." He adjusted his spectacles and gave a dry little chuckle before continuing. "Besides, it will be most entertaining to see how our so-called elite react to your behaviour. The highest-ranking lady amongst us is merely the daughter of a baronet. Even the governor general's wife holds her title only through marriage. While you, my dear," he said, turning to Caroline, "happen to be a lady in your own right. It is going to be extremely difficult for them to censure you."

"Then I shall be most happy to give them all a run for their money." Caroline laughed.

"Oh, do be careful, Caroline," Eliza Fairchild protested. "You really mustn't encourage her, Stephen. Your niece has a wild streak in her and is capable of doing the most extraordinary things."

"Such as coming out here on a wager," Caroline said frankly, knowing that her aunt had not disclosed any of that business to her brother when she had written to tell him of the proposed visit.

Stephen shook his head when he had heard the full story.

"Oh, dear . . . oh, dear . . . oh, dear . . ." The little man looked quite worried. "That was a most irresponsible act, niece. I had my doubts about your coming even for a visit. But I welcomed the idea because I did so wish to see you and for you to meet your cousins. However, I had no thought of your staying beyond the fall. I have grave doubts that even your aunt will be able to take our winters out here, but a young person like yourself will find it quite intolerable, I'm afraid."

"Well, the die is cast, Uncle Stephen. And whether you like it or not, I'm afraid you will have to put up with me until this time next year," Caroline said with rather more bravado than she felt. "I've no doubt that I shall be able to find something to help me while away the time."

"You will have no great difficulty there, niece, I'm sure. Apart from the invitations that are bound to pour in upon you, I'm afraid, as I have already said, you will have to do much more for yourself. In fact, if we are to entertain very much, you will find it inevitable that you do some of the chores yourself. Of course, all the ladies try to hide the fact that they have to help with the household work, but everyone knows it is quite impossible for the few servants we can get to keep a large house clean and tidy and do the cooking as well. And if there are children to look after, the tasks can become quite onerous."

As they prepared for bed that night, the two ladies talked over the events of the day. Eliza agreed with her niece that neither Mrs. Kendall nor her daughter had made a favourable impression. But it was obvious from the way she blushed each time she mentioned his name that Count de la Fayre had won Miss Fairchild's esteem.

Caroline was beginning to feel quite limp after all her exertions, and threw her gown over the back of a chair, saying that Hannah could see to it in the morning. But her aunt would have none of that. "You had much better begin as you are obviously going to have to continue," she said reprovingly. "With guests coming to dinner tomorrow evening, Hannah will have her work cut out helping Agnes with the cooking while poor little Mary does the housework. And I shall be busy looking after the children, for that is why I have come out here. If you do nothing else, you must learn to look after your own clothes, or you will end up without a thing fit to wear. You forget, it is not just a matter of sending for the milliner or taking a carriage to Bond Street every time you need a new outfit. What you have now will likely have to last you all year, unless you are prepared to become your own seamstress or use the local talent, such as it is."

The last remark shocked Caroline into shaking out her pretty gown and putting it away carefully. They had already agreed that though the ladies of York Town were quite handsomely gowned, the cut and finish of their clothes left much to be desired, and as for style, they were easily a year behind the times. Caroline went to bed vowing that she would not be seen dead in any of the fashions she had witnessed that evening.

"I thought Captain Chinery looked remarkably well turned out," Eliza said as they lay side by side in the dark (both having declared the bed was uncommonly hard after their soft mattresses back home). "But Stephen tells me that he makes frequent trips to see his parents in Boston, so I have no doubt he buys his clothes there."

"Some of them, possibly," Caroline mumbled sleepily. "But those awful clothes he was wearing yesterday morning were scarcely fit for a country yokel. It was no wonder I took him for a hired hand."

"Never mind, dear," her aunt said comfortingly, feeling that Caroline was embarrassed by her mistake. "I am sure the captain is a broad-minded young man and will overlook the error."

"Oh, I'm quite sure he will," Caroline replied. "He is more than capable of overlooking many of the social mores that we are accumstomed to. I have already discovered that."

"Really? Well, just try not to let it bother you too much. I'm sure we shall both get used to their strange ways in time, and his heart is in the right place." With that she gave a deep sigh and fell asleep.

Caroline, however, suddenly felt remarkably wide-awake. Possibly Pierce Chinery's heart was in the right place, but she was having grave doubts about her own. Never in all her young life had she been subjected to such treatment. The most audacious of her swains had never ventured further than to peck at her cheek when she wasn't looking, and they had quickly been soundly reprimanded for that. Yet this . . . this upstart had kissed her full on the lips, not once, but many times, and she had been quite incapable of calling him to heel.

Caroline stole out of bed, and crossing to the window, released the blind quietly for fear of disturbing her aunt. She stood there recalling the warm fierce pressure of his lips on her mouth and the bruising strength of his arms as he crushed her against his body, a body pulsating with a vitality such as she had never before experienced. His behaviour had been utterly despicable . . . contemptible . . . inexcusable . . . Caroline ran out of words with which to describe it. So she contented herself by leaning against the window, looking up at the stars hanging from invisible threads in the sapphire sky, and wondering how long it would be before he attempted to do it again—and if he did, what she possibly could do about it.

4

The following morning over breakfast, Stephen Fairchild suggested that if the ladies were willing to throw in their lot and help with the preparations, they might include Etienne de la Fayre and his niece in the dinner party that evening. Caroline and her aunt were more than willing. In fact, Miss Fairchild blushed very becomingly and began to flutter in a most unaccustomed manner.

"Very well," her brother continued. "Perhaps Caroline would care to ride over there with me this morning before I go to the office. It will give her an opportunity to see something of the countryside."

"Ride?" Caroline queried, remembering the mud.

"Yes, my dear. I understand that you are an accomplished horsewoman, and where they live there are no roads, so a coach is out of the question. I doubt if even a farm wagon could get through at this time of the year. In winter it is not so bad, as the snow and ice become hard and we can use the sleigh."

Caroline was not at all averse to the idea, but she decided that she would wear her brown woollen riding habit rather than the green velvet. Henry brought round a fine little chestnut mare for her, and the two of them set out along Yonge Street. A number of expatriate Frenchmen had settled along this main road to the North, but Stephen explained that the count had a small holding a mile or so to the west.

"I'm afraid he has cleared very little of his land. He is hampered by lack of funds and help. Poor little Anna does what she can, but cutting down trees is a man's work, and the count is far too old for that."

It was a beautiful sunny day, and Caroline was cheered to see that the mud was already beginning to dry out in many places. "Another week or so, and by the middle of May you will begin to see how beautiful this country really is. It can happen almost overnight, and by the end of June it can be so hot that the ground will be cracking under our feet. Of course we have to be careful then because of the forest fires."

Caroline was not too worried about his last remark, although she felt that he was inclined to give her hope with one hand and take it away with the other. But for the moment she was content to enjoy the ride and was quite impressed by some of the large estates she passed on the way.

As if reading her thoughts, her uncle said, "You must remember, when you are judging us, that York Town has only just been declared the official capital of Upper Canada. For a long time the government has been wavering between changing it to either Kingston or London. But now they have come to a definite decision, you will undoubtedly see some very rapid changes. I know several businessmen who have only been waiting for the news before entering upon new developments. As you can see, a great deal has already been done to clear the forest."

"They appear to have left a great part of it still in the ground even so," Caroline said as she skillfully guided her mount around the many tree stumps that peppered their way.

"That is another of our problems that has to be overcome. The settlers are responsible for clearing the road in front of their own property, and anyone sentenced for drunkenness is required to clear a stump, but it is a long job. As you can see, even those fields that have been cleared ready for sowing are sadly marred by fallen trees as well as stumps, which makes their cultivation extremely difficult. But clearing them is almost impossible—we shall just have to wait until they die off naturally."

They travelled at a leisurely pace to give Caroline the opportunity to become familiar with the landscape. Their journey led them past scattered farms, some of which were nothing more than a small log cabin with a barn nearby. But there were several larger houses, the tidiest amongst them belonging to the members of a Quaker settlement. Others stood empty and derelict, and Stephen Fairchild explained that they had belonged to a group of French royalists who, now that the monarchy had been restored, had returned home to France.

"Unfortunately that sort of thing frequently happens out here. People come for various reasons and then find they cannot take to the life. We have a very transient population, but there is a nucleus who are determined to stay and help in the development. Good morning, Caleb! I'm pleased to see you have at last found time to start clearing some of your frontage." Stephen had stopped to speak to a rough-looking man who had been working away at a stump.

Caroline had noticed him while they were some distance away. He had paused to rest on his ax for a while, but as they drew nearer he had deliberately set to work again with averted gaze.

"Aye," he replied. "Yon Pathmaster would give me no peace until I did."

"Well, we all have to do our share if we want our little community to progress. Caroline, this is Caleb Wallis, he used to work at Wheal Farrow," Stephen said, mentioning a tin mine near the family estate in Devon. "This is my niece, Lady Caroline Fairchild—or course you know the Duke of Walford, her uncle and my brother."

"Oh, aye!" Wallis said again but made no attempt to look up.

There was a definite chill in the air which Caroline tried to thaw by saying brightly, "You're a long way from Devon out here."

"So are you, m'lady. But I guess you didn't come because your uncle enclosed the land and turned you off your farm?" He swung the ax and left it deep in the stump before looking up into her face. "But I ain't sorry. There be plenty of good land out here if we can get our hands on it, and we will, given time." His tone and manner had softened a little, but Caroline sensed a kind of threat underlying his last statement, and her uncle appeared slightly embarrassed.

A young woman had come out of the cabin with a baby in her arms and another clinging to her skirts. "Is this your wife and family?" Caroline was about to dismount and speak to the woman, but Mr. Fairchild gave a warning cough, so instead she took a sovereign from the reticule she carried and handed it to the woman, who took it eagerly.

Caleb Wallis sprang at the woman. "Give it back, Alice," he said, tussling with her, but she was quick to slip it down the bodice of her gown. With an angry snarl he brought the back of his hand across her face, and turning to Caroline, put a restraining hand upon her bridle.

"I'm sure you meant it kindly, ma'am, but she don't need your charity. I provide for her and her brats."

"They're your children too, Mr. Wallis," Caroline looked him steadily in the eyes, although her heart was pounding against her ribs.

"Only the boy . . . the young'un. The other I feed out of charity."

"Then you can hardly fault me for assisting you in your good deeds," Caroline responded sharply. "Now, if you'll kindly take your hand away, we'll be on our way."

Caleb's shifty eyes slowly travelled over the slim figure on the horse, pausing on the little pearl-and-ruby brooch that pinned the lace cravat at her throat and the gold fob of her small pocket watch. He took his time, but eventually he lifted his great coarse hand and raised it to his cap in a dilatory form of salute.

Neither of them spoke until they were well out of earshot. "I'm sorry you should have been subjected to that," Mr. Fairchild said. "He's a surly fellow at the best of times, but I've never known him to be so impertinent. I was afraid you were going to strike him with your whip."

"So was I," Caroline replied. "Not so much for his impudence, but that poor woman looked at death's door."

"I'm glad you didn't strike him. He deserved it, I know, but the people out here would not take kindly to such behaviour. The lower classes are jealous of their newfound freedom."

"Then they had better learn to use it responsibly," Caroline said, but the incident had unnerved her. At home, in England, her rank alone would have been sufficient to inspire respect and a certain amount of awe, at least to her face. It was true in recent years the hoi polloi in the big cities had been given to attacking their betters, but only when supported by a mob.

"Did you suspect he'd do such a thing? Is that why you warned me not to get down off my horse?"

"No, I was as surprised as you were. But I didn't want you to go near her. She has what is commonly termed out here 'a graveyard skin.' I fear she has not long to live, her lungs are quite gone."

"All the more reason why she needed the money and why that big brute should have kept his hands off her. What did he mean 'only the boy' was his—did he marry a widow?"

"I doubt if he's married her at all. A great many couples don't bother about a ceremony out here, often because there is a dearth of preachers. However, in his case, he may have a wife and family back in England. When he's saved enough to bring them over, he'll throw her out but keep the boy to work the land."

"The duke would never have allowed that amongst the people on his estate. If that's what freedom means, then I think it needs to be curbed."

Her uncle sighed. "To make a system of government such as ours work, I'm afraid there has to be trust and responsibility on both sides, and unfortunately, we are all guilty of abusing it, even those amongst us who should know better." They continued on in silence for some distance.

"What I cannot understand, uncle," Caroline said as they entered a dense stretch of forest, "is why they have chosen to settle so far apart from one another."

"That is another of the touchy problems that I was mentioning to you last evening. You see, a great deal of the best land has been set aside for the Church, which is why it is called the clergy reserves. But the Church, having neither the money nor the inclination to develop it, leaves it in its natural state. This means that vast tracts of land such as we are passing through at the moment are not available to the settlers, and they are forced into isolated areas. A fact which is making a number of them very angry."

"Men like Wallis, you mean?"

"Not only him. Pierce Chinery and a number of the younger men in our society are beginning to feel that there should be a change. They also feel that the revenue of the country should be under the control of its people."

"Having seen this, I can sympathize with them," she said.

Stephen Fairchild furrowed his brow and looked across at her anxiously. "Do be careful to whom you make such a comment, my dear. The Reverend Mr. Strachan and John

Kendall are extremely powerful men and wield a great deal of influence. They will not hear of dividing up the reserves, and I'm afraid the situation is becoming quite explosive."

"I can imagine it would be if Captain Chinery had anything to do with it." She laughed.

Her uncle was not inclined to comment on that remark, and for the rest of the way Caroline had to be content to learn about the flora and fauna of the Home District, as that area of Upper Canada was known. He explained that the best land was where the maple, basswood, and beech trees grew; where the pine and hemlock were plentiful, there was too much sand.

By the time that they arrived at Count de la Fayre's small log house, Caroline had already learned enough to recognize that the land surrounding it was unlikely to yield much in the way of a harvest.

As they rode through the opening in the rail fence, Etienne de la Fayre came forward to greet them. He bowed gravely before holding Caroline's horse and helping her to dismount. She had had too much on her mind to pay more than scant attention to him the night before, except to notice that he was quite distinguished and that his dress clothes were more than a little out-of-date and shabby. This morning she could see that beneath his thick mane of white hair and small pointed beard he was quite fragile. But his clear blue eyes looked at her unfalteringly, and he had retained all the gallantry of his youthful days at the French court.

He was wearing the heavy grey garb Caroline now recognized as being common among the settlers, but his hands under their coating of dirt were fine-boned like those of an artist or a musician. His breathing was shallow and his face ashen from the effort of clearing away the underbrush, but he welcomed them with all the aplomb of a nobleman escorting honoured guests into his château.

"Anna," he called as they entered the single living room of the log house. "Anna, we have guests."

His niece hurried out of the kitchen wiping flour from her hands as she came. She too was dressed in a coarse grey woollen dress, with a little kerchief tied over her hair.

"Please excuse me," she said as she bustled to see them comfortably seated and provided with a decanter of wine and glasses. "But I am making bread today, and as we hardly ever have any visitors, I was not prepared."

Caroline hastened to set Anna's mind at rest by admiring

the many little feminine touches to the otherwise plain furnishings. Then, while the men were busy talking, she asked if she might go into the kitchen and watch her at work.

"The bread smells delicious," Caroline said as Anna reached into the brick oven with the long-handled wooden peel and brought out the steaming-hot loaves. "But how did you ever come to know how to do all these things?" She indicated the spinning wheel in the corner and the evidence of many other tasks that Anna was obviously in the habit of performing. "I simply wouldn't know where to begin."

"Of course not," Anna replied without any trace of resentment. "But then, you are a lady and were not born to do such menial work."

"Neither were you," Caroline protested vehemently.

Anna looked across at her and gave one of her gentle smiles. "Thank you, Lady Caroline."

All the slights and anguish the girl had suffered underscored her words, and the thought of the way she had been treated by a group of snobbish females made Caroline's temper rise.

"I would like you to call me Caroline, and I shall call you Anna. And one day perhaps you will teach me to make bread, for I'm sure it must be fun playing with all that dough."

"I should like that very much." Anna gave a wry grin. "But as to its being fun . . . I suppose it would be if you only did it on occasions just for amusement. Unfortunately, there is always so much to do on a farm, and there are only my uncle and I to do everything."

"You mean you work on the land as well?" Caroline said in a shocked tone.

"If we didn't, there wouldn't be anything to harvest in the fall."

"But don't you have anyone to help you at all? Surely you have a hired man to work the land for you?"

Anna shook her head. "When it comes to harvesting, they are all busy with their own crops, or they hire themselves out for more money than we can pay. Sometimes one of our neighbours will take pity on us and spare a few hours to help Uncle Etienne with the tree felling. We have to clear at least two acres a year if we are to be allowed to keep it." Putting her last batch of bread in the small oven, Anna picked up a log basket. "Will you excuse me for a moment," she said before going out to the woodpile in the backyard.

Caroline got up from the pine stool on which she had been sitting and wandered around the small kitchen. She stopped to look at the blue-and-white china on the dresser, then crossed over toward the window. Her attention was suddenly taken by the sight of a second figure near the woodpile, and she drew back behind the chintz curtain.

The stocky figure of Chad Kendall had just stolen up behind Anna and placed his fingers over her eyes. The young girl gave a delighted squeal, and before you could say "japonica" she was in the young man's arms and he was kissing her. He did not exude quite the same passion as Pierce Chinery had done under similar circumstances, Caroline noted with satisfaction, but it was perfectly obvious that it was not the first time such a thing had occurred.

Not wishing Anna to think that she had been spying on her, Caroline walked into the living room to join her uncle and the count. Stephen Fairchild remarked that they should be on their way, and how happy they were that the count and his niece would be dining with them that evening.

Just at that moment Chad Kendall appeared at the front door, having come round the other side of the house. He greeted them all, including Anna, as though he had just arrived. Caroline, knowing what she did, decided he was an extremely poor actor. The others of course suspected nothing. But Chad was a likable young man, especially now that he wasn't tied to his mother's apron strings, and if Anna liked him, that was sufficient for Lady Caroline.

Her eyes glinting mischievously, she said, "Uncle Stephen, may we include Mr. Kendall in our little party tonight? It will round out our numbers very nicely and give Anna someone else to talk to."

Her uncle looked a trifle surprised but quickly hastened to proffer an invitaton, which Chad accepted with alacrity. Then, having made their adieu, they set their mounts toward York Town. As soon as they were out of range, Stephen Fairchild looked across at his niece and said, "Now you have really set the cat amongst the pigeons, Caroline."

Caroline's amber eyes had an expression of bland innocence, although she already had some idea of what might be coming. "Oh, Uncle Stephen, don't tell me that Mr. Kendall isn't on your visiting list?"

"Certainly not!" Her uncle was horrified at the mere suggestion. "John Kendall is one of our most influential citizens. He and his family are accepted by all the elite.

Although," he added ruefully, "I must admit that I am not greatly enamoured of the man. He has all the arrogance of the *nouveau riche*."

"Then what is troubling you?" Caroline said, setting her mare to a brisk trot so that her uncle should not see her laughing.

"My dear," her uncle said breathlessly while whipping his horse to keep up with her, "Have you any idea of what Mrs. Kendall will say when she knows her son is dining with Anna Thomas?"

"But he isn't. He's dining with Mr. Stephen Fairchild," she replied lightly.

"You know I can't help feeling that you are deliberately mistaking my meaning, Caroline," her uncle said, drawing alongside her. "I told you last night that Anna is merely tolerated. And that means that we are always very careful to see she is never invited when any of the top families are present, unless it is an assembly of some kind."

"Really?" This time Caroline's voice was tinged with anger. "How very hypocritical, especially as Chad Kendall is in love with her." Ignoring the shocked expression of her uncle's face, she went on to tell him what she had just witnessed.

"I find it hard to believe . . . not that I doubt your word, my dear. But I cannot imagine what would happen if the news were ever to get about."

"Why, they would get married, of course. And in my opinion, they would make a very good match. Chad is cut out to be a farmer, and Anna would make him an excellent little wife. With some of the Kendalls' money, they would be able to develop that place, and it would make life easier for the count."

"Oh, I agree most heartily. There is nothing I would like better. Chad is a very nice fellow, even though he is not very bright. But his father is set on his becoming a lawyer and is already arranging for him to be given a good position in the government."

"Then I'm very much afraid that Mr. John Kendall will have to make other plans, and he had better include a new daughter-in-law amongst them." Caroline set her delicate little jaw at an angle that her aunt would have immediately seen as a storm warning, but Stephen had yet to learn to recognize the signals.

"No, my dear niece, you may put such an idea right out

of your head. Such a match would never be allowed, of that I am quite sure. I can only hope that Chad will be discreet and not let the cat out of the bag about Anna being present at our little get-together this evening."

Caroline would have liked to add that she hoped Chad would be man enough to make up his own mind on such a personal matter as marriage. But having no wish to cross her uncle, for she was already becoming quite attached to the timid little man, she chose for once to hold her peace. Instead she settled down to observe the sights and sounds of her surroundings in greater detail.

The first thrill of discovery having passed, she was suddenly aware of the vastness of this new land. They had covered only a few miles, but this merely served to reinforce the fact that beyond her immediate horizons lay vast tracts yet to be explored. The size of everything alone filled her with awe, and the terrain was far rougher than the gentle hills and dales of the English countryside; even the little streams gushed and swirled around the outcrop of rocks with a kind of hidden fury, as if resenting anything that might hamper their progress. There was a savage beauty about it all, heightened by the thought that within the cool dark depths of the forest wolves, bears, and other creatures, unknown or long forgotten in Europe, still made their home. And the giant trees towering above her, their branches entwined in Gothic tracery, had a disdainful pride that fought the very ax that felled them. This land would not surrender its soul easily to the hand of man.

"I have to make a brief call at the Red Lion Hotel," Stephen said as they neared the outer limits of the town.

"Are you starting to imbibe so early in the day, uncle?" Caroline teased. It amused her to see the shocked expression on his face as he quickly protested such an idea.

"We use the tavern as a polling place for our elections, and since space is short, we hold some of our meetings there. I assure you, my dear, I merely have to go there on official business." Mr. Fairchild had reined in his horse in front of a square white clapboard building sporting a large swinging sign of a ferocious lion rampant on a red background. Tying his mount to the hitching post, he said, "I shouldn't be above a few minutes, but be advised, my dear, the place is crowded with farmers, as you can see and hear, so stay near to the window where I can see you."

Caroline nodded absentmindedly. Her attention had been caught by the animated roarings of a crowd somewhere at the back of the building. No sooner had her uncle gone inside than she turned her horse and trotted round to see what it was all about. The area surrounding the tavern was covered with an assortment of carts and wagons through which she had to thread her way. It would have been easier on foot, but the mud and a certain innate caution prevented her from dismounting.

In a small clearing at the back, a few yards from the tavern itself, there was a crowd of some fifty or sixty men. It was impossible for her to see what they were watching with such noisy intensity, but every so often a shout would go up interspersed with cries of: "At him, fellow! Sic him, boy!"

Caroline waited and watched for a moment until she was able to distinguish other sounds: the heavy breathing, the thudding, and the growls and whimpers of dogs fighting. She hesitated for a moment before touching her little mare lightly with the whip and trotting at a pace into the throng.

The men fell back startled to see a stranger, and a woman at that, in their midst, and let her pass in a sudden silence until she reached the centre. Caroline closed her eyes, for the sight that met them was almost more than she could bear. A great bull mastiff, enraged by taunts and gibes, his hide pricked by the onlookers' sticks, held a small terrier in its jaws. It was impossible to see the colour of the small creature, for it was little more than a ball of raw flesh and blood.

The mob shifted uneasily, and the sudden silence that came upon them at Caroline's arrival caused the giant dog to pause in his attack. He stood there glowering at her, blood dripping from his mouth. She was no stranger to blood sports, but she had always refused to be in at the kill, and now she realized why. Never had she witnessed such savage cruelty. She recovered herself, and raising her whip, lashed out at the dog, which, unnerved by the unexpected fury of her attack, dropped his victim and backed away, leaving a bundle of limp ragged bones upon the mud. Caroline looked down upon it as it lay twitching on the ground, its only remaining eye pleading for help.

She turned on the silent throng. "If there's a man amongst you, you will kill it," she said, "and put it out of its misery." But no one moved. The excitement having passed, many dropped their heads and began to shuffle away. The owner of the mastiff had gone to find his dog, which stood shivering on the outskirts.

"Here . . ." Caroline reached into her reticule and produced a small pearl-handled pistol she always carried for her protection. "Use this." She proffered it around, but no one came forward to take it from her.

"You kill it, ma'am. You stopped the fight or it would have been all over before now." She looked across and saw that it was Caleb Wallis who had spoken. He was watching her, a glint of triumph in his narrow eyes.

"It is a man's job." Caroline tried to stop her voice from faltering. "But it seems there is no man here."

"This is a man's sport. You had no business to stop our pleasure."

"What pleasure can you find in such uneven odds? Even a fair fight would have been disgusting, but in this you are no better than the dumb animals themselves. Have none of you a sense of fair play?" Her words caused even more of the men to move uneasily away. Only a half-dozen or so now remained to enjoy her obvious discomfort. The dog at her feet whimpered and tried painfully to struggle to its feet, but collapsed with an agonized cry of pain.

She stared across at Wallis and saw that he was waiting eagerly for the moment she would have to back down and turn away. He was enjoying the anguish written on her face. Caroline braced herself. Never in her life had she knowingly killed a living creature, and the thought of it was almost unendurable. Had the primeval savagery of this country permeated the very heart of the people? She dismounted and braced herself; then, taking aim, she squeezed the trigger and shot the terrier between the eyes. The small body convulsed and then lay still. She lay back against the neck of her horse and closed her eyes in a silent prayer both for herself and for the life she had just taken. But she opened them in a flash as she heard Caleb's footstep in the mud.

"Don't take another step," she said. "I've killed once today. The next time, it will not come so hard. In fact, I might almost find it a pleasure." She aimed the pistol at his heart, and he fell back.

"I was about to help you remount, m'lady," he said, and there was a new note of respect in his voice. "I must say I never thought you had it in you."

"Neither did I," Caroline replied. "But I'm discovering

we never know what we can do until we are put to the fence—so do not tempt me." She swung herself up into her saddle and rode away to where Mr. Fairchild, his face grave with anxiety, was hurrying to meet her.

"That was a foolish act, my dear," he chided her gently, noticing how her hands were trembling.

"I know," she said, "and not the first of which I'm guilty. I seem to be given to such folly." She whipped up her horse and cantered briskly away, leaving him to follow as he would.

5

By the time they arrived back at King Street, Caroline had begun to recover some of her spirits. She had elicited a promise from her uncle not to mention the affair at the Red Lion Hotel, knowing her aunt would be scandalized by her part in it, however well-intentioned. But when told of the morning's events at Count de la Fayre's, Eliza Fairchild supported her niece wholeheartedly.

"I'm surprised at you, Stephen," she said. "You were never so spineless as a boy. You know perfectly well that Anna has all the characteristics and manners of a lady. And just because a few ill-bred colonials consider her mother married beneath her, there is no cause for you to support them. It would do well for them to remember that the poor child's father was injured defending their liberty."

"She hasn't changed one jot." Stephen sighed as his sister swept out of the room. "She had a terrible temper as a girl, and she used to take me to task unmercifully." He turned and looked at Caroline. "And I'm very much afraid that you, my dear niece, have inherited the worst of her traits. But I must say," he added with a twinkle in his eye, "life was never dull when Eliza was around. It is just that I have become very set in my ways, and being alone, there was no one I could draw on for support."

Caroline leaned over and kissed the top of his bald head

before going out to see if she could help her aunt with some of the preparations for what looked to be a very entertaining evening.

Anna and her uncle were the first to arrive, and Caroline noted that the poor girl was wearing exactly the same dress as she had worn to the assembly. She took her up to her bedroom to freshen up after the journey, and while there, she said, "Anna, would you think it very presumptuous if I were to suggest a new way of dressing your hair?"

At seventeen, Anna was as intensely interested in fashion as all young ladies of her age. "Oh, please do," she begged. "I have no ladies to advise me, and of course I know nothing of the world of fashion."

"Then we shall make a pact. I will tutor you in all the latest modes and help you with your wardrobe, if in return you will teach me to become a housewife and do my own baking."

A happy smile spread over the girl's face. "I've already pledged myself to that, Caroline. Although I'm sure that in your position you will never need such skills."

"My Aunt Eliza has always told me that in this world you can never be sure of anything. And I can tell you, Anna, one can become just as bored with a life of leisure as with that of continual work. So it is agreed that from now on we shall share our talents," Caroline said, kissing her to seal their newly forged bond of friendship.

The Anna that went downstairs to greet Chad Kendall looked vastly different from the timid little miss that had but recently gone up with Lady Caroline. A cherry-coloured sash about her slim white dress with a matching knot of rosebuds nestling in the curls of her new hairstyle had quite transformed her both in appearance and in manner, although the latter change was due in part to the fact that she could claim Lady Caroline Fairchild as her friend.

Pierce Chinery was also waiting to meet them, and his eyes lit up with pleasure as he noted the change in Anna. But his attention quickly turned to Caroline, who was looking ravishing in a pale green batiste gown.

"I can see that a good fairy has waved her wand over little Anna," he whispered as he led her in to dinner. "I am so pleased, the poor child has so few pleasures in life." He gave Caroline's arm a warm squeeze and winked at her audaciously. "You know, ma'am, from all I see and hear, I have a strange feeling that we may well prove to be two of a kind, you and I."

"If that should prove to be the case," Caroline replied with a touch of irony, "we shall have to be careful not to lock horns."

"That could happen only if we were of the same sex." He grinned wickedly. "And you, Carrie, are certainly not built like any man I know."

"The name is Caroline," she reproved him, feeling that she should at least make some attempt to keep him in line. Truly he was quite irrepressible. "But tell me, Captain Chinery, what is it that you have heard of me?"

"That you faced down a mob of farmers outside the Red Lion today and threatened Caleb Wallis with a pistol."

"Who told you this?"

"Dan Logan, my hired hand. He was amongst the crowd, and said you put them all to shame. Your conduct's made him think again about the value of so cruel a sport. He is a kind man of himself but tends to follow where the loud ones lead."

"I'm discovering that we can all be guilty of that. Too often we conform to the rules and habits set by society without questioning them."

"If you've discovered that, you have indeed made strides. It is a pity that some of the gentlemen in this community do not share your views."

"You do not think such behaviour unbecoming for a lady?"

"How can what is honest or kind be unbecoming to anyone, regardless of rank?"

"Then you suggest that I should always speak my mind?" Caroline gave a wistful smile.

"If what you say is prompted by what you feel in your heart. And provided always that you think before you speak." Pierce eyed her saucily. "It is my firm belief that we are all intended to use what brains we have to the best of our ability. And at a guess, I would say you have a great ability."

"So you would have no objection to a woman challenging you at your own game, then, sir?" Caroline's amber eyes twinkled. "What if she beat you at it?"

"If she could do it with style, I hope I would have sufficient class to acknowledge her my equal. And if it were with you, ma'am, I should most certainly enjoy the skirmish."

Caroline pursed her lips to prevent herself from laughing. "Unfortunately, you have the advantage. For too long we women have left the important decisions to the men and have allowed ourselves to be no more than playthings."

Pierce threw back his head and laughed so heartily that all heads turned in their direction. "That you could never be, Caroline. I, for one, would as soon play Russian roulette with a loaded pistol."

Caroline was exhilarated by their verbal duel and happy when her aunt suggested they should round off the evening with some music. It gave her the opportunity to display her hands and her virtuosity at both the piano and the guitar, and later the whole party joined in a general sing-along, with plenty of laughter from all present. Finally Pierce picked up the guitar, and strumming his own accompaniment, sang an old Canadian folk song, interspersing each of the verses with a merry whistle, all the while casting impudent glances toward Caroline.

There was a wee farmer who lived in this town,
And he tore up the groun', the devil knows how.

The devil came up to him one day
Saying, "One of your family must come my way."

"O, surely it's not my eldest son,
For if it is I am undone."

"Oh, surely it's not my eldest son,
It's your scolding wife, and she must come."

He hoist' the old woman upon his back
And like a bold peddler he carried his pack.

Oh, in he came to hell's back door;
He threw her in upon the floor.

Up stepped a little devil a-rattling a chain;
She upped with her leg and knocked out his brain.

Up stepped a little devil behind the wall,
Saying, "Take her away or she'll kill us all."

Oh, women they are worse than men
They'll go down to hell and come back again!

When he finished, the ladies laughingly protested at the words, which they considered a slight to the fairer sex. But Pierce had a pleasant light tenor voice and a merry roughish grin, so that it was impossible for anyone to really take offense. But, as Miss Fairchild sagely remarked, "At least the poor woman survived the adventure. And out here, survival itself is a virtue, I would think!"

"I couldn't agree with you more, ma'am," Pierce said, becoming strangely grave all of a sudden. "It just ain't any good, a woman coming out to these parts, unless she has the stuff of survival sewn into every seam of her." He had set the instrument aside and was standing by Caroline, who had been attempting to accompany him at the piano until the speed of his singing had become too fast for her.

"And some of them, through no fault of their own, just ain't cut out for it," he continued in his soft, slow drawl. "Take Caroline, now." He picked up one of her delicate white hands from where they rested on the ivory keys. "This is a mighty pretty little hand, and a sight softer to touch than any you would find out here 'cepting the older ladies'. But I'd sure hate to see it after it had been using an ax."

For some unexplained reason his words stung, and Caroline snatched back the hand he had been holding so gently, saying, "In England we have servants to do such work. We have better things to do with our time." She could have bitten her tongue the moment the words were out, but they had the desired effect.

"Yes, I guess you do, ma'am. Your world is a way different from ours. Over there you go and watch the wild animals in a cage. Out here we have to learn to live with them, and I doubt if you see much difference between them and us." The expression in his eyes and the cold tone of his voice sent a sudden chill along Caroline's spine. In its way, it was more scaring than the howling of the wolves. It was as though he had suddenly resolved something in his own mind, and because of it, she felt a sense of loss.

Shortly after that, the party broke up. Count de la Fayre and Anna had some miles to go, and Chad offered to ride with them part of the way. Pierce bade his host and Miss Fairchild good night. Then, coming to Caroline, he picked up the offending hand and raised it to his lips in the most courtly fashion.

"I'm sorry if my remarks offended you, Lady Caroline, it was not my intention. There are many kinds of beauty, and each requires its own setting; yours undoubtedly belongs in a London salon. Please excuse me and put it down to the rudeness of a backwoodsman." He gave a formal little bow, and turning to Hannah, took his tall beaver hat and swung his cloak about his shoulders. He looked the very essence of gentilly, standing there with the soft candlelight playing on the silk frills of his shirt. He gave another bow to everyone in general and strode out into the darkness.

Caroline had a desperate urge to run after him and try to mend the rift that had plainly come between them. Yet her pride held her back. From an innocent remark the whole incident had blown up so quickly into something quite serious, and she knew not how. But it was the first time she remembered Pierce Chinery using her title when addressing her, and for some ridiculous reason she resented it far more than she had his so resolutely refusing to do so before. She went to bed that night feeling miserable and confused. Some inner sense told her that when Pierce walked out of the door that night, he had also made up his mind to walk out of her life, and that was something she couldn't allow to happen, for like it or not, he had taken her heart with him.

6

April soon gave way to May, and with each succeeding week Caroline found herself taking on more and more of the chores. She certainly had no time to be bored. Agnes had left, and Hannah was trying to cope with the cooking and the marketing. Miss Eliza saw to the children, mending their clothes and attending to their many needs, while Mary did her best to keep the house spotless and see to the laundry. Finding the child nearly dropping from exhaustion on one occasion, Caroline had valiantly attempted to help with the ironing until she burnt a large hole in one of her uncle's best shirts and Mary begged her to leave it be.

All of this was an entirely new experience for her ladyship, and she was often irritated to find herself incapable of simple menial tasks. "I swear if I stay here much longer, I shall have lost all faith in the superiority of the upper classes," she told her aunt one day.

"I have pondered upon that myself," Miss Fairchild said reflectively. "I cannot help feeling that it would be more sporting if each man or woman were to earn his own laurels."

"I know I shall have far more respect for the tweeny at Walford House when I return," Caroline said, brushing some stray hairs from her face. She was hot from sweeping the veranda and steps, a job she had voluntarily undertaken to save Mary. "I'm certain that, dressed in my finery, she would be able to decorate a salon with the best of them, but I doubt one of my friends capable of setting out a line of washing like that." She pointed to several rows of sheets blowing briskly in the warm spring breeze.

"I think that, given the opportunity, a great many of them could learn, as you are doing, my dear. The fault is not so much within them but in the arbitrary rules of society that force them into such an idle life."

"It's quite ridiculous," Caroline said. "As I told Blanche Kendall the other day when she caught me helping Henry to groom the horse, I would far rather be worked to death than bored out of existence."

Miss Fairchild was amused to see the vigour with which her niece attacked each new task. "I'm afraid you're causing quite a pother amongst many of the young ladies out here. Nevertheless, remember, my dear, this is new and something of a game to you; I shall be interested to hear your views on the matter in a few months' time."

"You sound like D'Arcy Letton. He was certain I would never be able to stand it."

"Heaven forbid that I should ever share an opinion with that man." The thought horrified Eliza. "A great deal of success depends on how much your heart is in what you do. At the moment, you are happy to be here, but if that should ever change, then everything you are forced to do will become a burden to you."

"Yes, I suppose you are right—you usually are." She kissed her aunt lightly on the forehead. Miss Fairchild was sitting in a rocking chair patching a pair of breeches for Mark. Caroline's thoughts had turned to Pierce Chinery. There had been no sign of him since that night of the dinner, although her uncle had remarked that he had seen him unloading goods at the docks. And on one occasion his business among the settlers had given him cause to ride out past the captain's farm.

"This is one of the busiest seasons of the year," Mr. Fairchild had said. "Everyone is busy with spring planting. But come the summer and you will find we shall return to some of our more social activities."

Frequently Caroline would accompany Hannah to the market, as that poor woman became quite flustered when it came to bartering, and the odd assortment of currency in use left her in a complete haze. Her ladyship's quick brain could more easily assess the honesty of the people with whom they traded. Most of them were open and helpful, happy to teach her the finer points of selecting a chicken or a hog, once they got over the initial shyness of dealing directly with someone of her rank. But there were some who resented it. She could read the suspicion in their faces, not least among them Caleb Wallis. She had seen him several times on market day. If Alice was with him, she would always smile and curtsy, and Caroline would stop to pass the time of day, but Caleb always scowled and walked away. He was a great uncouth hulk of a man around thirty or so years of age, given to sulking in corners with others of his like.

She mentioned him to her aunt one day, omitting the circumstances of their first meeting. "Caleb Wallis—that name rings a bell in my memory," her aunt replied. "I seem to recall some trouble at the mine. I'll think on it."

Shortly after that, Mr. Fairchild took to his bed with a severe attack of ague, a common complaint in those parts, due to the mosquitoes that bred in the large swamp on the outskirts of the town. When it at last began to abate, Miss Fairchild herself looked fit to drop. She had insisted on keeping the night watch and refused to let the others do her daily tasks.

"I think you need a change," Caroline said one morning. "We both do, come to that." For in spite of her aunt's protests, she had tried to take as much as possible off that good lady's shoulders. "I propose that we drive out to see Anna . . . and the count," she added, knowing Miss Fairchild would find that a tempting bait.

"Henry cannot possibly be spared as things stand at the moment," her aunt responded wistfully.

"We don't need Henry to drive us. I know the way, and I'm more than capable of taking the reins, you know that."

"I know that you're capable of anything once you set your mind to it."

"Then it's agreed. We'll start out first thing tomorrow and be back before the children return from school. I'll get Hannah to put up a basket of goodies for Mrs. Wallis. When I saw her at the market last Saturday, she told me the babies were ailing sadly and she feared it was the fever or worse."

"Then I hardly think it wise for you to go near them, my dear. In any case, from what you have told me, I hardly think Caleb Wallis is likely to welcome your interference."

"I'm not thinking of him. It is Alice and the children I wish to help. He has no thought of anyone but himself."

It was a bright June day and the buds on the wild roses that lined the ravine were showing the first signs of opening. "It is unspeakably beautiful," Eliza said, "in spite of its wildness. I wonder if man will ever be able to tame it... which will be destroyed, the country or the men?"

"You forget there are the women. Perhaps they will keep the balance," Caroline said, bringing the calèche to a halt near Caleb's cabin. She had to stop some distance away, because he had done nothing more toward clearing the road since that first day.

Alice came round the corner of the cabin. She had been to the woodpile, and her arms were full of logs, but she dropped them and hurried forward to greet them.

"Oh, my lady, I'm so pleased to see you," she said, her face grey with care. "I'm afeared the little 'un be dying, but I'm not knowledgeable in such things and don't know what I should do."

"Stay here, Caroline," Miss Fairchild said. "I've seen more sickness than you, and if you cannot help, there is no sense in your running an unnecessary risk."

Caroline recognized the tone of authority in her aunt's voice and knew it was pointless to argue. "Very well, aunt. But you will call me if there is anything I can do." She turned away and wandered over to the small stream that ran nearby. She could just see the door of the cabin through the trees and could easily hear if her aunt should call. She knelt to pick some wild yellow daisies growing along its edge. There were no flowers in the garden at King Street as yet, and she thought they would brighten her uncle's sickroom. She had not picked above a dozen when she heard a noise in the bushes behind her and turned to see Caleb Wallis towering above her.

"That be trespass," he said, grinding the remaining flowers into the ground with his boot. "Your uncle would 'ave 'ad me transported for less."

"That he would not," Caroline said, rising to her feet indignantly. "The duke's tenants were at liberty to pick wildflowers wherever they chose. And if they were sick, he would send armfuls from his gardens."

"Very kind of 'im, I'm sure. It did a lot to fill their bellies. Pity he was not so kind with poachers."

"He did not like thieves any more than I. And you know it is against the law for any but the squire or his heir to hunt game on the estate. He would have been the first to send food if he knew it were needed."

"But he didn't know because 'e wasn't there 'alf the time, was 'e?" Caleb thrust his face forward, and she caught the strong smell of liquor on his breath. "And anyway, we don't want charity from the likes of you."

"There was no need for charity if you had a job at Wheal Farrow. He was noted for always paying a fair wage for a fair day's work, even if other employers were not." Subconsciously she edged away and wished she had remembered to bring her reticule, which she had left lying on the seat of the carriage.

"Maybe, but 'o's to say what is a fair day's work? And what if a man don't want to work? Maybe 'e'd sooner dally with a dollymop like you." Wallis shot out his arm and grabbed her wrist, thrusting her back against the rough bark of a tree. "I bet a lady like you could pleaure a man well if she'd a mind to." He leant against her, his hulking body pinning her against the tree. "I'll take this for a start," he said, fumbling one of his hands about her waist and wrenching the little fob watch from beneath her spencer. "And then I'll think what else I'll be having." He leered at her, the sweat and spittle drooling down onto her breast.

Caroline closed her eyes and tried to clear the sensation of blood swimming in her head. She opened her mouth to scream, but he slammed her shoulders back against the tree, expelling the air from her lungs in a whimper.

"Where's 'er ladyship's pride now, eh? No, you wait my pleasure," he said, roughly banging her hand back against the bark and scraping the flesh as she tried vainly to free herself from his grasp.

"You could be hung for this," Caroline managed to mutter between clenched teeth.

"You'd never dare." Caleb laughed coarsely. "What, tell all your fine friends 'ow you was dishonoured by the likes of me? No . . . you'd never do that. Now, if it was one of your young bucks, that'd be different, wouldn't it?"

"No, they'd still hang."

Caleb shook his head and laughed down into her face. "You could never send a man to the gallows. It cost you all you got to shoot my dog . . . you could never send me to be hung by the neck until I was dead. Or would you bring all your smart friends down to see me dancing and kicking at the end of a rope?"

Caroline tried once more to scream. This time Caleb raised his hand and struck her across the face as he had done to Alice that day. The blow split her lip, and she felt a trickle of blood run down her chin. Grabbing her wrist, he flung her upon the ground. "Go on, be off with you . . . I'd get more pleasure from a tavern doxy. I'll not waste my time prigging the likes of you. Think on that, yer ladyship. Caleb Wallis would sooner ride a common whore." He spat in the grass beside her and turned to walk away.

"Caroline!" She heard her aunt's voice calling from the direction of the house, and she scrambled to her feet. Her gown was torn and filthy and her hair had fallen about her shoulders. Caleb turned and looked at her, his eyes smouldering.

"My aunt . . . she's looking for me," Caroline spluttered, afraid he was going to change his mind and attack her again. "She has been tending your child."

He bowed mockingly and swept his arm to show her she could pass. "Tell her," he said, "and see me hung and Alice and the children starve."

Caroline hurried past him toward the cabin. "I'm here, aunt," she called, wiping the blood from her face with her gown.

"Great heavens, child! What has happened?" Miss Fairchild paused in what she was about to say.

"I was . . ." She looked up and saw Caleb daring her to speak. "I was climbing those rocks by the stream and fell . . . and Caleb Wallis came my way."

Her aunt's face showed her dismay, but she had other matters on her mind. "Mr. Wallis," she said, "you should be with your wife, your son is dead."

Caroline sensed more than saw the arrogance flow out of him. Without so much as a look at either of them he strode toward the small cabin. "It isn't easy for any man to lose his son, but I have little pity for him." Miss Fairchild stared after him. "His wife had sent him for help early this morning. I'm sorry for her, but he deserves the misfortune that has befallen him, from what I can see. And now"—she turned her attention to her niece—"that was a very nasty tumble you took. How careless can you be!"

"It's nothing a good bath and a little liniment won't mend."

"A needle and thread are also called for," Eliza said, eyeing the torn gown despairingly. "You were always a tomboy, Caroline, and it seems you haven't changed. Come, let's go home and bath ourselves. I've no wish to carry infection to our own children. The count and Anna will have to wait for another day."

But whether it was the shock of the baby's death or the strain of nursing her brother, the following day Miss Fairchild herself was far from well, and the doctor diagnosed the ague and sent her packing off to bed.

Caroline had little time during the next week or so to dwell upon the incident with Caleb Wallis, although at night it often haunted her dreams and she would awake stifling her screams, afraid she might disturb her aunt.

Anna arrived one day to find Caroline next to tears. Hannah was feeling unwell, and although she had stoically tried to cope with her work, the heat of the kitchen had proved too much for her. So Caroline had sent little Prissy to minister to the needs of the invalids while she tried to master the mysteries of cooking.

Expertly Anna set about organizing the evening meal. The two boys would soon be coming home from school, and Caroline was well aware that their first need would be for something to eat. Under her young friend's gentle guidance she quickly discovered the intricacies of preparing vegetables and making pies.

"I could never bring myself to do that," she said, having watched Anna kill and pluck a chicken. Caroline was nursing a burned hand because she had disregarded her friend's advice to use the peel when removing the bread from the oven.

"I'm sure that you could do anything you turned your mind to, Caroline. Just look how you have turned a moth into a butterfly," Anna replied happily, the feathers flying around her. She was referring to the remarkable change that Caroline had encouraged her to make in her own appearance. "Mrs. Kendall passed me in her carriage the other day on her way into town. Usually she tries not to see me, but the new bonnet you helped me decorate is such an eyecatcher that she was forced to take a second look. And then she actually had the good grace to acknowledge me."

"So she should," Caroline retorted sharply. "But what about Chad? I'm much more interested in seeing him behave like a man and pay court to you openly." The girls had been meeting frequently, and it had not taken long for Caroline to admit to what she had seen, merely to reassure Anna that Chad Kendall was plainly in love with her.

Anna blushed prettily. "I'm afraid you set too much store by that notion," she said. "I haven't much hope of anything more coming of that relationship, for though Chad often declares his affection for me, he has never once mentioned the question of marriage. I fear his family would never agree to it."

"You would be marrying Chad, not his family," Caroline said with some irritation. "Though I must admit that I would not care to have Blanche Kendall for my sister-in-law." Before her aunt and uncle had taken to their beds, they had endured the entire family of Kendalls on two occasions. Once when they were invited to dine at the large brick Kendall town house full of ugly tasteless furniture; and then when the visit was returned. Afterward both Caroline and her aunt had warned Stephen not to be in a hurry to accept another invitation from that quarter.

That evening after Anna had gone and everyone except Caroline was in bed, she sat gazing out of the big window over the backyard. The lawns at home would be carefully tended and the flowerbeds a mass of blossom. Out here there were too few people and little time to tend to such luxuries. Any energy or inclination they had in that direction was turned to producing food. But at last the buds on the maple were beginning to open and the delicate fronds of the willow were turning green. Caroline had never before realized how much joy she found in watching leaves on a tree unfold.

The episode with Caleb had left its scars. Not physically; the scratches had been only superficial, and the dirt had soon been washed away. But the bruising she had received to her spirit was something new. At one time her pride and anger would have acted as a shield, but now they did not suffice against this unprovoked attack. Caleb's coarseness, his rudeness, even the blow did not distress her as much as his desire to deliberately shame and destroy her as he had crushed the small wildflowers under his boot. She had never been subjected to such mental stress before, and she had no way of knowing how to deal with it. She longed to be home, away from this wild uncouth land, back among the ordered rituals of a society with which she was familiar. For that moment she took refuge in planning the garden. Tomorrow she resolved to have words with Henry; she would ask him to dig over the ground so that she could plant some flowers. One way or another she was determined they would have an English flower garden to gaze out on.

The sun was setting over the lake, streaking the sky with fingers of deep rose. Caroline set aside the mending she was attempting to do for the boys and sat there staring out into the distance, trying to visualize the preparations for the new season that would be going on now back home, but that only led her thoughts to D'Arcy Letton. It was odd, but in a strange way Caleb Wallis and Letton seemed to have something in common: D'Arcy also had a wish to destroy, whether it be with pistols in a duel or the cutting edge of his sarcastic wit. How could she ever have found him amusing? Caroline shuddered at the thought of having to spend the rest of her life with him, and it deepened her resolve to stay.

She had begun to lose some of the fear she had first felt at the size and wildness of the country; there were moments when she almost felt a part of it, but loneliness was her greatest enemy. The only way anyone could stay over here and keep her sanity was if she were part of a family. No, it was more, even, than that, for she did have her aunt and uncle and her small cousins, holy terrors though they might be. For her to be willing to stay in such a place, there would have to be a stronger bond than affection; she would have to marry, and that was out of the question. Besides, having taken stock of the young men of any account, she had come to the conclusion that there wasn't a suitable one amongst them.

It was becoming embarrassing, though. For their part, there were several who refused to give up heart as far as she was concerned. Oliver Rowlands was a most persistent admirer and always calling on one pretext or another. The children were always pleased to see him, because he usually came armed with large boxes of candy that Caroline immediately handed over to them. But the man was an arrogant snob, far worse than Letton and not half as intelligent. What was more, Caroline considered that he was an extremely bad influence on Chad Kendall, who it turned out was his cousin on Mrs. Kendall's side of the family.

There was only one man who had awakened any interest in her, and he had disappeared into the underbrush, or so it would seem. Anyway, Caroline refused to let herself think about Pierce Chinery. He had been quite right—her place was not here—and as soon as the period of her wager was up, she would return to civilization.

She must have fallen asleep, or was so lost in reverie that she did not hear the front door open. The next thing she was aware of was Pierce's voice calling her uncle's name. She rose quickly from the chair and turned to greet him as he entered the room.

The last rays from the dying sun gave her hair a halo of burnished gold, and the sight of her standing there made Pierce hesitate before stumbling over his apology. "I'm sorry to intrude on you like this, ma'am. But I have just heard that Mr. Fairchild and your aunt are laid low with the fever, and I came to pay my respects and see if there was anything I could do to assist."

"Oh, please do come in and sit awhile, Pierce." His first name slipped out easily, for that was how she always thought of him now. "My aunt and uncle are in bed, and now Hannah is far from well. I packed her off to bed as soon as the children were asleep."

"So that was why I got no reply to my knock. I was just thinking that the whole family must have hightailed it back to England," he said with a laugh. Then, looking down at his coarse working clothes, he remarked, "I'm hardly attired to sit here in the parlour, ma'am."

"That doesn't matter. I should be glad of your company for a time, especially if you will agree to be less formal and call me Caroline."

Pierce relaxed and grinned as he came across and sat facing her near the window. He had obviously been a little apprehensive about his welcome. "That will be my pleasure," he replied, noticing with some concern how much the role of nurse had taken its toll upon her. Caroline had lost a deal of weight and was looking far from well herself.

After inquiring how he was getting along with his spring

sowing, Caroline, reflecting her own thoughts, said, "It must be lonely for you out there in the evenings."

"I love the wilderness," Pierce replied. "And it's not nearly as lonesome or as quiet as you'd think. There's always the howling of the wolves to keep me company." He laughed boyishly at the remembrance of the night outside the garrison. Caroline dropped her head and blushed with embarrassment. "But then, I was kind of born to it, although my folks live in the city. They could never make me out, because as soon as I got out of school or college, I would take off for our farm, away from all the hustle and bustle of Boston. I can see it would be different for you, because there are occasions when it suddenly hits me, and the loneliness becomes almost more than I can bear."

"You'll have to take a wife . . . even if she goes to hell and back," Caroline rejoined laughingly.

"Oh, I fully intend to, just as soon as I've finished a house to bring her to. A man can't manage alone out here. Besides, he needs sons to help him on the land. But she would have to be a gal born and bred to the life," he added with a note of wistfulness in his voice.

"I've no doubt you will find a stalwart woman who will be able to fight off all the devils for you," Caroline said lightly, feeling that perhaps the drift of their conversation was becoming too personal.

"It's not so easy. You know what the Good Book says: 'A man does not live by bread alone.' I'd need someone with brains as well as brawn before I'd be content to spend the rest of my life with her."

"Isn't there anyone back home in Boston?" Caroline inquired innocently, although it was a question that had frequently entered her mind during the past few weeks.

"No one special, but some who might do," he replied casually, as though he were discussing the merits of some cattle. "The trouble is, they don't want to leave their homes and family and come out west."

"What made you decide to come so far away?"

"Well," he said in his slow drawl, "I ain't so pleased with what's happening back there. There's getting to be too many people, and now they've started building factories. I can see that in a very few years it will be every bit as bad as London, England."

Caroline had just grown used to them always adding the

name of the country when they spoke of a town or city in Europe, because so many settlers, feeling homesick, had named their new towns after those in their native land. "I take it you didn't care much for England, then?" She tried to sound casual, but at the moment Pierce was treading on very sensitive ground.

He must have guessed at the thoughts passing through her mind, for he hastened to qualify his statement. "Oh, don't get me wrong. I sure as anything loved the countryside over there, but I'm not a city boy, whether it be London or Boston. And I sure as anything got mighty tired of trotting up and down . . . what's the name of that place in Hyde Park?"

"Rotten Row," Caroline supplied the missing words, smiling as she did so.

"Yes, that's right. But I ain't cut out for ambling along all done up in my best bib and tucker and doffing my hat to anaemic young ladies passing by in the carriages. I'd as soon get on my horse and let him go like the wind, over the hills and far away."

Watching his eyes, Caroline thought she could see an endless horizon, as though he were looking at worlds beyond her ken. And she was suffused with an intense longing to share them with him. But she said, "What makes you think you are the only one who likes to ride like the wind? There is nothing I like better. During a hunt I'd take a fence with the best of anyone."

"Is that so?" Pierce raised his brows. "Then I guess it wouldn't be out of place to ask you to go riding with me as soon as I've finished my planting."

Some of Caroline's old spirit was returning now she had someone to talk to. "I'll do more than that," she said. "I'll wager I can beat you over any distance you care to name . . ." She suddenly stopped short and caused Pierce to look at her inquiringly. "I'm sorry," she said. "I made a wager once, which I'm already regretting, and I've vowed I'll never make another."

"The stakes were that high?" Pierce watched shrewdly, awaiting her reaction.

"Yes," she replied, turning her gaze away lest he should see the anxiety in her eyes. "My aunt has always told me a lady should never gamble. I should have listened to her." Then, wishing to change the subject and realizing that she had not offered him any refreshment, she hastened to do so.

He accepted the offer of some wine, and as she handed him the glass he caught her hand in his own strong one and turned it over, examining her many scars.

"I was right. These pretty hands were not meant for hard work—they scar too easily."

"It's nothing," Caroline answered, drawing back quickly. "I have merely been amusing myself learning to cook. Anna is a splendid teacher—she is going to make someone a superb wife, if only he will make up his mind and stand up for her like a man."

"So you've guessed about Chad Kendall?"

"I didn't have to guess. It's written all over his face every time he looks at her."

Pierce laughed. "I've heard my mother use that tone of voice whenever she was measuring up prospective suitors for my sisters. It has the ominous tone of a matchmaking female."

Caroline tossed her head. "And I suppose you don't hold with it. Well, let me tell you that if I do nothing else during my stay in Canada, I have every intention of seeing those two married before I leave."

Pierce lay back in his chair and applauded, his eyes twinkling merrily as he said, "But I do agree with you most heartily. Chad has often mentioned it to me, but there is little that I can do about it other than tell him to stand up for her like a man. As you are probably already aware, like Anna, I am not included in their tight little circle. They are willing to tolerate me rather more kindly because I am a man and my financial status is better than the count's. Although I have my doubts that will last much longer, for I have had just about all I am willing to tolerate of the way they are running this province." The grey eyes had suddenly darkened to the colour of thunderclouds, and Caroline was astonished by the fierceness of his tone.

"Then let us do our best to undercut them," she said, trying to defuse the anger of his glance. "For I can think of nothing more likely to deflate the Kendalls' pride quite so much as having to admit Anna to the bosom of their family."

"Done!" Pierce said, taking her hand and kissing it gently. "Now I must be on my way. But make your plans, you conniving wench, and I shall be at your side to help you."

7

The following days were hard for Caroline. Hannah was forced to take to her bed, and although her aunt and uncle were improving, they were far from well and rest was essential to their full recovery. If it had not been for the kindness of Stephen Fairchild's friends and neighbours, life would have been quite intolerable, for she had only little Mary to help her look after the invalids as well as the house and children. But no one was more amazed than Caroline at the way she soon began to cope with the many problems.

"This bread is truly delicious," Anna said, tasting a new batch Caroline had just removed from the oven. "I can tell that before many more weeks have passed you will have far outstripped me with your culinary prowess."

"Never!" Caroline laughed as she proudly displayed a cake she had made for that evening. She did not mention that it was for the sake of Pierce Chinery, who had promised to look in and see how they were all faring. "My efforts vary with my inclination, and I all too quickly become bored. But I must say that I would never have credited myself with the abilities necessary for the running of a household such as this. At home I always had an abigail to attend to my least whim, and I realize now that that took all the incentive away. I shall certainly play a more active part in caring for myself when I return."

Anna looked crestfallen. She had become deeply attached to her fiery young friend. "You fully intend going back to England? You wouldn't be content to make your home out here with us?"

Caroline looked across at her and smiled. She too had grown very fond of Anna—she who had never been one to form a deep friendship with anyone other than her aunt. "I think I will have to go, Anna. I was not born to such a life, and after a time I would become crotchety and ill-tempered in such a small society. Many of them already play on my nerves until I could scream every time they come near." She was thinking of the Kendalls and Oliver Rowlands in particular.

"But York Town is growing so rapidly, and there will be other people coming in to join us. I think it is only because you have met so few that you feel like that. The country folk are far more warmhearted than the six or seven families that consider themselves the elite. As soon as you can leave some of your chores, you must come with me and meet some of them."

Anna's sentiments were echoed by Pierce that evening. He had come into town especially to see Stephen and play a game of chess, for Mr. Fairchild was now sufficiently recovered to sit in a chair upstairs in his bedchamber. But although Captain Chinery gave that as the sole reason for his visit, he managed to dispatch his obligation with remarkable speed. This enabled him to spend a considerable time downstairs with Caroline, sipping wine and partaking of her freshly baked cake.

"You have been shut up in this house far too long. Summer is under way, and the countryside is the only place to be in weather like this," he said solicitously. Caroline was looking very pale and tired and could easily come down with the fever herself. In fact, he had been so concerned about her that he had insisted on her taking a dose of her uncle's medication of wild black cherry steeped in whiskey. She had protested violently, but Pierce had threatened to hold her down and force her to take it if she did not oblige, and she knew he was more than capable of carrying out his threat.

"As soon as Hannah is up and about again, I am going to take you off into the woods for a picnic," he said emphatically.

Caroline gave him a roguish grin. "Really, Captain Chinery, do you have any idea what that would do for my reputation?"

"In this society, you would no longer have one. But you are well aware that I would not suggest such a thing. I was thinking that Anna and Chad could come with us, and if Miss Fairchild felt well enough, she might follow us part of the way in the carriage. She could rest at my place while we explore the hills beyond. Don't forget, you have still to prove your ability as a horsewoman, but if it is anything like your ability as a cook, then I am prepared to take your word for it," Pierce said, helping himself to another piece of cake.

Caroline was strangely torn by the conflicting emotions she was experiencing. She was pleased and flattered that Pierce should remark on her cooking, and proud of her achievements in that direction. But at the time time, as she had frequently done over the past few weeks, she saw a certain absurdity in the situation. She could just imagine how many of her acquaintances in London would find it a cause for merriment that she, Lady Caroline Fairchild, should be playing the role of cook, nurse, and housemaid combined. D'Arcy Letton would never let her live it down were he to know about it.

She glanced up and found Pierce watching her. It seemed that he was able to read her mind, as she had discovered he so often did. "Never mind, Lady Caroline, at least when you return to your life of leisure you will have learned to appreciate the skill of your cook."

His tone was pleasant enough, but again Caroline resented the use of her title. She felt that he was setting her apart as someone alien to him and to the country that he loved. And though she was constantly battling with herself about it, Caroline knew in her heart that she wanted to be a part of it. No, that wasn't strictly true. She wanted Pierce Chinery, but not here in this godforsaken country with so few people, and none of them her own kind. However, one lesson she had learned over recent weeks was not to react too sharply to such remarks. Pierce would only become frigidly polite and walk out in a huff, leaving her feeling lonely and wretched. If she was compelled to stay in Canada for another nine months, then she at least wanted to stay on friendly terms with him. He was the only one who made her life there at all congenial.

It was not long after that visit that they were able to go for their strawberry picnic, because life at Stephen Fairchild's suddenly took a turn for the better. Her uncle, who was fully recovered, returned from the docks one morning looking very pleased with himself.

"I have a surprise for you ladies," he said. "I met an acquaintance of yours. I was told that a person had been asking around for the Fairchild residence, and I decided to seek her out." Both Miss Fairchild, who was now strong enough to come downstairs, and Caroline were agog to hear his news.

It turned out that Bridget Ryan, whose son Caroline had been concerned for on the voyage, had just arrived in York Town. The poor soul had suffered a great misfortune since they had last seen her in New York. Her husband, Anthony, had died of typhoid on the journey to Upper Canada, leaving her almost destitute. She had had no choice but to continue on, hoping to find employment for herself and the two older boys, Patrick and Sean; the baby, Tony, was no more than a toddler.

"Sad as it is for the poor woman, I think I was able to lighten her burden. I have engaged her to come here and help Hannah, and rented her that small cottage I have on the edge of town. I've also promised to try to find suitable employment for the boys. They seem a most excellent family. Just the type we need to settle in these parts."

"Oh, they are," Caroline and her aunt cried in unison, relieved both for Mrs. Ryan and for themselves.

"We noticed she did her best to keep the boys spotless throughout a most trying voyage," Miss Fairchild added, "and that was no easy task."

"I could see that she was a very tidy body and not afraid of hard work. Her only concern is to make a new life here for her children. She seems determined to make a success of it. It is a great pity that all our settlers do not share that view. I also saw someone else with whom you are acquainted. Caleb Wallis was in the stocks. I always find that a most distressing sight. The only thing worse is a public whipping or hanging." Mr. Fairchild shook his head at the thought.

"Caleb Wallis!" Caroline repeated the name. Her thoughts immediately flew to the theft of the watch, and she wondered if he thought she was to blame. "Of what was he accused?"

"Sedition," her uncle said gravely. "He was addressing a crowd of farmers outside the Red Lion, urging them to violence against the legislature. Demanding the people should take over the government. The high constable arrested him, at great personal risk to his own safety, for Wallis had inflamed the mob. He came up before John Kendall, who has no sympathy with anybody preaching dissent. He sentenced Wallis to six months' imprisonment and two hours a day in the stocks."

"And a good thing, too," Miss Eliza said. "While I can see many things that need righting out here, we can do it without violence, I'm sure. And I dread to think what would become of us all if Caleb Wallis and his like were in charge. I'm only sorry for his wife and child."

"Yes, what will become of them?" Caroline asked. She felt guilty to find her heart lighten at the thought that Wallis was shut away for the next few months.

"Some of our citizens are generous enough to contribute to a fund to help the destitute. I will make it my business to see what can be done."

Within a few days after that, Mrs. Ryan had settled in and was fast becoming one of the family. So it was that on a fine hot morning in late June, Caroline and her aunt, accompanied by Chad Kendall, set out along Yonge Street toward the Count de la Fayre's homestead. Chad and Caroline were on horseback, but Eliza, with Henry up front, was in her brother's calèche and complained bitterly about the journey over the bumpy logs of the corduroy road across the swamp. She was still fragile from her recent bout of fever and had not fully regained her normal high spirits. Even so, Caroline had noticed that a change had come over her aunt in recent weeks, especially whenever the name of Etienne de la Fayre was mentioned.

The count, like his niece, had been one of their most frequent visitors, and whenever he came, most of his time and attention were directed toward Miss Fairchild. Eliza, in turn, had become as moody as any young girl in love, and when Caroline had teased her on the subject, she had protested vigourously that the idea was quite ridiculous; she was far too old to think of such things. Although she added a rider that for his age the count was remarkably well preserved and exceedingly good company. It was at the thought of seeing him, rather than acting as chaperon for the girls, that Eliza had agreed to come that morning. That was certain, for Hannah could now have undertaken that task.

Pierce had arranged to meet them at the count's place, and then they were all to proceed to his farm, where he had arranged for them to lunch. Anna joined the others on horseback, while the count, much to Caroline's amusement, said he would accompany Eliza in the carriage—a statement that immediately brought about a transformation in her aunt's mood.

"Mrs. Logan has put up a remarkable picnic for us," Pierce said, reining in his great black stallion alongside Caroline's small mare. "And I have asked her and Daniel to set it up alongside the stream, where there is plenty of shade."

The Logans, he had already told her, now rented his original log cabin and acted as housekeeper and hired hand.

"You are lucky to have such good servants," Caroline remarked as they led the small party through the dense forest, pausing occasionally to help Henry with the carriage whenever the road narrowed excessively.

"I don't think upon them so much as servants," Pierce replied. "They are more like family. Besides, as soon as my house is finished and I have set up housekeeping for myself, I have promised them enough land to start their own homestead. They have no children, so they are happy to stay nearby, fortunately. That way we can help each other, turn and turn about."

Caroline still found it bewildering that he should so easily speak of his hired help as though they were his equals, but she had learned that nothing provoked him so quickly as for her to comment on it. Rather she decided to make the most of the situation and tell him of Mrs. Ryan's problems.

"I could certainly use the help of the older boy if she is willing to let him go from home," Pierce said quickly.

"He's little more than thirteen years of age and nothing but skin and bone," Caroline replied. "I doubt if the child had a good meal in his life until Hannah set one before him the other day."

"You know, Carrie, I find it difficult to make you out. You have the warmest heart in the world about creatures less fortunate than you, yet you refuse to acknowledge them as being your equals."

Another thing that Caroline had come to realize was that whenever Pierce called her Carrie, he was in one of his provocative moods. What she had failed to note was that this often coincided with the times she was looking her most ravishing, as she was this morning. Any man would have been a fool not to have desired such a woman, and Pierce Chinery was no fool.

"It is not a matter of merely acknowledging them as being equal—that wouldn't help in the slightest. Surely you can see that it is a fact of life that we are all born to our particular station in the world and there is nothing that we can do about it. That doesn't hinder me from wishing to ease their lot in life whenever it comes my way to do so."

"But not to alter it. To let them take their place alongside you?" Pierce questioned.

"It is not in my power to do that. We are governed by the law of God and society. All men were, unfortunately, not created equal, no matter what you Americans may choose to think."

"Oh, don't worry, we have plenty who think just as you do," Pierce said somewhat scathingly.

"Well, I'm very pleased to hear that they haven't all lost their sense of fitness," Caroline snapped back, setting her little horse to a gallop, for they had come to a wide clearing. In spite of the fact that the captain's horse was the larger by several hands, the little mare was lighter and carrying less weight. Also, having the advantage of surprise at the start of the race, Caroline reached the top of a steep rise well before Pierce.

"There!" she said, smirking in a most unladylike fashion. "I have beaten you." Pierce had dismounted, as the others were some distance behind them.

"Maybe," he replied. "But don't forget, the race is not always to the swift. Anyway, you cheated and must pay a forfeit." Suddenly he had swept her from the saddle into his strong arms and was kissing her with all the passion of the parched land yearning for the rain. The abruptness of his action had prevented Caroline struggling, and now the ardent fervour of his kiss robbed her of any desire to do so. Then, just as swiftly as he had held her, he let her go.

Setting her back in the saddle, he said with a note of bitter humour, "You have paid your forfeit, so you may go. I must not take more than my due; I must always remember my station in life." He turned away to remount his own horse, and Caroline was thankful he did not see how his words had brought tears to her eyes.

"That isn't fair of you, Pierce."

"It was just as fair as the way you started the race," he said laughingly, but his eyes were not smiling.

"You know perfectly well that I wasn't referring to you. You are a gentleman born and bred. That you chose to ignore the fact doesn't alter matters. This may be the New World, but a gentleman's place in it has not changed, whatever you think."

"Then it's about time it did," he countered sharply. "I'll grant you that a gentleman is born, whether it be in a settler's cabin or a duke's mansion. And it's high time we started to acknowledge a man for his worth to the community rather than his manners in society." A pair of amber and a pair of grey eyes glowered at each other fiercely, neither of their owners willing to give one inch in the positions they held.

"It has nothing to do with a person's worth," Caroline said stiffly. "As I said before, it is entirely a matter of birth and breeding."

Pierce sat back in his saddle, put his hands on his hips, and tossed his head in a gesture of incredulity. He was looking remarkably handsome in an open-necked, full-sleeved white cambric shirt and tan breeches matching the cuff on his fine black leather riding boots. "Then, ma'am," he drawled, "will you be so good as to tell a poor colonial boy just why you bother your pretty head over defending the rights and privileges of Anna Thomas? Because I sure as heck can't understand your line of reasoning."

"Then you obviously wasted your time at university. It is as plain as the nose on my face, and perfectly logical," Caroline said with the utmost confidence.

"Pish!" Pierce dissolved into a gale of merry laughter. "In the first place, the nose on that pretty face is far from plain, and you know it. In the second, you are willing to go through hell fire and face Mrs. Kendall's wrath because you think, and rightly so, that Anna is worthy of your regard. Come, my dear Carrie, let's not quarrel on such a lovely day. I can hear the others approaching. You see that oak down yonder . . . ?" He pointed to the valley below. "I'll give you a head start and race you there, provided that when I win I can claim another kiss."

Caroline was sensitive to the fact that she had not won her verbal battle with him, and angry with herself because this would be a race she was more than willing to lose. But she tossed back her hair, her bonnet having already fallen and hanging by its ribbons around her neck. "I've told you I no longer wager. . . . And you have yet to win." With that she spurred her horse to such a gallop that Pierce was again taken by surprise.

She was away like the wind, and he was far more intent on watching her skill with the reins than spurring his own horse to overtake here. Nevertheless he refused to be beaten a second time, and in a moment they were neck and neck. He reached the old tree a shade ahead of her, but she had not reined in her horse and continued on, taking the small creek that lay before her with an easy jump.

"Bravo!" Pierce applauded with genuine admiration, for although the stream was narrow at that point, a little higher its white water whirled and eddied over some rocks. The sight and sound of it would have daunted most young ladies of his acquaintance.

Caroline should have been pleased, but at the moment she chose to find his praise patronizing. Turning her horse, she trotted upstream to the rocks. It was much wider here, and she drew back to take a longer run at it. Pierce called to her to stop such foolishness, but it only succeeded in making her the more determined. Leaning low over the neck of her little mare, she whipped it on, sailed into the air, and landed neatly on the other side, where Pierce was waiting for her.

The challenge had quite eradicated any anger she felt toward him, and she laughed up into his face, but the grey eyes were like thunderclouds. Far from congratulating her, he turned his mount and cantered back toward the carriage rumbling across the plain.

"The road out here is in remarkably good condition compared to some areas I have seen, Captain Chinery," Eliza Fairchild said as the carriage drew alongside. "Most of them are little more than narrow dirt tracks."

"Naturally we are favoroured, ma'am," Pierce replied caustically. "Both the Kendalls and the Pagets have farms near here, so they have seen to it that we are well served in that respect."

"But doesn't your local administration see to such things for you?"

"Oh, they see to it, but for themselves in the main. As to representation, we have a town meeting once a year to elect a warden, poundkeeper, and a postmaster, along with some other minor officials. Even then, the few families that hold the real power make sure that their man is elected."

"You sound very bitter, captain." Eliza gave a half-smile, hoping to soothe the obviously angry young man. "Don't tell me you too are a revolutionary, for the world has seen enough of that kind of thing in the past few decades."

"No, ma'am. I don't entirely hold with it myself. I believe that all men are created equal, but after that, it is up to them to fit themselves through education and experience to become our leaders. But I consider it the responsibility of our leaders to see that the people get the opportunity to do just that."

"Don't tell me that Pierce is boring you with his political theories," Chad Kendall said as he and Anna joined them. "I've told him that he should go into politics himself and bore the legislature instead of his friends," he continued good-humouredly.

"You know you agree with me, Chad, so why not be man enough to say so openly?" Pierce said curtly.

Chad's pleasant young face flushed with embarrassment rather than anger. He genuinely admired Pierce, but he was tied too fast to his family's apron strings to stand out against them. "I'll speak up when the time is right," he said. "Come, Anna, Pierce's place is just over that rise. Let's beat them to it."

The two of them went on ahead at a brisk pace, but Pierce made no attempt to leave the side of the carriage, so Caroline was forced to follow behind on her own. It was almost midday, and except when they were in the shade of the trees, the heat was almost unbearable. Eliza was sheltered by a large parasol the count was holding over her, but her niece was hot and sticky from her exertions. She tried to rearrange her bonnet, but the bronze curls had escaped their bonds and were cascading over her shoulders.

A pox on them all! she thought as she drew her horse over to the creek and dismounted. Kneeling, she let the cool clear water run over her hands before splashing her face with it. Feeling much refreshed, she then proceeded to take a comb from her reticule and tidy her wayward locks. She was not concerned with time; the others could go or tarry as they chose. And as for Pierce Chinery, she didn't care whether she saw him again or not. She was so put out by his behaviour that she was of two minds whether she would turn back.

She was just rearranging her bonnet and thinking how she would enjoy returning to civilization where she would have a maid to attend to her toilet when she heard the pounding of hooves on the parched earth. Looking up, she saw Pierce galloping toward her, his fair handsome brow furrowed with anxiety as he scoured the landscape. Caroline stood up from the bank where she had been sitting under a clump of trees, and he suddenly caught sight of her.

As he reached her side, he sprang off his horse, and taking her by the shoulders, he shook her until her teeth chattered and her hair once more tumbled down over her shoulders.

"You little fool" he said angrily. "This is the second time today that you have scared the wits out of me. And this time it was your aunt and the others as well."

Caroline's amber eyes blazed back at him as she struck him smartly across the wrist with her riding crop. "Captain Chinery, kindly take your hands off me. I'm not accustomed to such behaviour."

"Well, you had better become accustomed to it, for it would seem to be the only way to make you aware of the dangers you run. Don't you realize that these forests on either side of you house a dozen different dangers. They are full of wild beasts, and not all of them walk on four legs. The men in these parts are not all saints."

"Really!" Caroline replied coldy as she remounted, trying to avoid his assistance. "I was under the impression you thought they were, and that you were their leader." As she trotted off up the rise, she tried not to think of the expression in his eyes. Once again her temper had got the better of her, and she was already regretting it, for beneath his anger she had read concern such as you show only for those you love.

The afternoon passed quietly enough. Anna and Chad made the most of their opportunity to be together, and wandered around the farm content in each other's company. Eliza Fairchild and the count likewise enjoyed being together, and the heat becoming too much, they retired to the coolness of the house, which left Caroline and Pierce to entertain each other. And in their present mood of hostility toward one another their scope for enjoyment was somewhat limited.

"Would you care to look over the house?" Pierce inquired after Mrs. Logan, a cheerful little woman, had cleared away the luncheon things from the rough wooden table set outside near the stream.

Caroline was hoping that he would make the offer, for she was entranced by the long, low building in the shape of a letter E, the centre being an attractive wooden stoop already entwined with flowering vines. She had heard Pierce telling her aunt how he was building onto the original log cabin of a former settler, which of course accounted for the fact that a great deal of the land surrounding it had already been cleared.

"I intend to set the fence well away from the house when I've finished, to allow room for a flower garden. As you can see, there are already a number of small beds in flower."

"I suppose they were here when you came?" Caroline said, thinking it unlikely that a man would bother with such delicacy, having so much rough work to do.

"No," Pierce replied. "My mother loves her flower garden, and I guessed it would be nice to have one waiting when I bring a wife to live here. I brought many of the plants along with me from Boston." His manner throughout was cool and detached, and Caroline found it impossible to liven the conversation with any semblance of warmth.

The interior was still in some disarray. Most of the walls had been plastered, but only the library was finished. Here the furnishings were rough and masculine, with shelves of books lining the walls and an astrolabe standing in the corner under the window alongside a desk.

Caroline fingered the books, noticing with interest that they contained the works of many of her favourite writers, including Lord Byron. "I can see why you would want someone with brains as well as brawn," she said laughingly, quoting him. She hoped he would be drawn out of his present black mood, for she was missing the fun she had come to have with him on his visits to her uncle's. But he seemed to resent her presence here, although he repeatedly asked her advice as to the decorations he should choose.

In answer to her remark, he said, "It is what I had hoped for, but I'm rapidly coming to the conclusion that the fairer sex were given beauty instead of brains, so I shall have to content myself with that or remain a bachelor. If I could rely on servants, I would prefer the latter."

Caroline bridled at his last words. "If you should ever decide to seek a wife, then I would suggest that you do not let her know you are merely looking for unpaid hired help. It is hardly flattering." She was quite relieved at that point to hear Miss Fairchild calling that they should be starting their return journey.

Count de la Fayre and Chad, supported by Miss Eliza, insisted that with Henry they afforded the ladies adequate protection and that it was pointless for Pierce to return with them. Much to Caroline's chagrin, he did not press the point, so she was forced to ride home with Anna and Chad, the latter accompanying them back into town.

"What is the matter, my dear?" Eliza Fairchild inquired while they were in their bedchamber changing for the evening meal. "It has been a quite enchanting day, yet on the occasions I have looked at you, I have seen thunder in your eyes."

"I am pleased you found it so congenial. For my part, I was heartily bored. Country ways are not mine, and for two pins I would return to England this minute, even if it means marrying D'Arcy Letton."

With a merry grin Miss Fairchild picked up the two pins that had been fastening her bonnet. "No sooner said than done," she said, offering them to her niece. Adding hastily, "It is a good thing that I have learned not to believe everything you say, especially when you are in a temper, but I despair of ever making you think before you speak. I suppose that is what happened between you and Pierce Chinery today, for I have never seen a more stormy couple in all my born days. And the poor man looked perfectly wretched as we drove away."

"That was relief at seeing the last of us, for I'm sure from what he said that he thinks all women are addlepates. He is looking for a wife who is as strong as an ox so that he may have dozens of sons to help him look after his precious land—while she drags out her days in the kitchen. If she weren't so old, I swear Hannah would make a perfect mate for him."

Eliza Fairchild made no attempt to reason with her niece. In such a mood, Caroline would only become more and more rebellious and inevitably end up hurting herself more than anyone else.

This in fact was exactly what happened. Caroline, in her blind anxiety to hit back at Pierce, took to encouraging the advances of Oliver Rowlands. She was in no way unseemly in her manner, nor did she stoop to playing the coquette. But if she happened to meet him while out walking with little Prissy, as was her wont, she made a point of stopping to speak rather than merely acknowledging his greeting. And if by some happy chance there should be any friends of Pierce Chinery's around, she was all the more animated in her conversation, hoping the news would be carried back to him. On one occasion he actually passed them on horseback. He bowed stiffly in acknowledgement, but Caroline was unable to tell from his expression whether he gave any account to the fact that she was talking with Rowlands.

Her friendship with Anna blossomed, as did Anna's with Chad. The girl herself was like a newly opened flower. She no longer hung back waiting for people to speak to her, and amongst the young ladies of York Town, she was rapidly becoming popular—with the exception of Blanche Kendall, of course.

Mrs. Kendall still cherished a fervent hope that Chad would be able to capture Lady Caroline Fairchild, and did everything to encourage a friendship between the two girls. Even to turning a blind eye to the fact that Anna Thomas was now being accepted in their little set.

As her uncle had promised, the summer proved to be a vast improvement upon the early spring. Week after week of long sunny days with hardly a cloud in the clear blue sky. True, there were many occasions when both Caroline and Miss Eliza Fairchild found the heat somewhat overpowering. But it was a delight to be able to plan ahead for outings, knowing that rain was highly unlikely. Although Miss Fairchild confessed that at times a fresh English shower would be most welcome to cool everything down, including people's tempers.

For the ladies who could afford to take time out and rest during the excessive heat of the day, sitting out on their stoops watching their tiny world go by and gossiping with their friends, life was not too hard. However, the majority of men, woman, and children had to continue their toil, and especially in the evening, when the taverns were full, the temper of the populace became like a tinderbox; the slightest spark would set it aflame.

There were frequent brawls, and rarely a morning went by without a new face appearing in the pillory or at the whipping post, the culprit having raised a ruckus the night before. Stephen forbade the older boys to venture out in the evening. Unfortunately, while a great deal of the damage was being done by roughnecks passing through to the cover of the backwoods and the North—ruffians of the worst kind, who were not averse to robbing an honest citizen of his money or property—they were not alone in this. The sons of principal families were known to amuse themselves harassing the townsfolk or encouraging others to do it for them. It was impossible to deal with these fellows, as they had their families to protect them, but Stephen Fairchild was determined that his boys should not become associated with their like. As Caroline and her aunt were finding, their neighbors were for the most part good, kindhearted people struggling against an untamed wilderness, hampered by lack of tools and supplies. However, it is rarely you find a barrel of apples without a few rotten ones in it.

8

As Stephen Fairchild had foretold, summer brought a renewed round of social activities. There was an outdoor assembly in the grounds of the garrison, but much to Caroline's disappointment, Pierce Chinery failed to attend. However, Oliver Rowlands was most persistent in his advances, so much so that she became quite uncomfortable whenever they were left alone together. Her only consolation was that Oliver's behaviour obviously annoyed his aunt. Poor Chad was caught in the crossfire of all this activity.

"My mother is most anxious that you should attend a picnic she is giving out at our farm next week," he said to Caroline during one of his frequent visits. The two of them had grown quite close since Chad had come to realize that it was not by chance that Anna nearly always happened to be there. "She told me to ask you first, before she sends a formal invitation, because she thinks you won't refuse if I ask you. I'm afraid she imagines that my frequent visits to you mean that we are becoming something more than friends," he added plaintively. "Not that I would object to that, of course," he hastened to explain, thinking he might have sounded rude. "But, as you know . . ."

Caroline smiled sympathetically. "Your affections are otherwise engaged," she finished the sentence for him. A flush spread over his broad face, and he dropped his head in embarrassment. "It's all right, Chad. You know you don't have to explain anything to me. Why, Pierce Chinery and I have been your allies in this affair. But you know the time is coming when you really must stand up and speak out, for I have no intention of standing by and seeing poor little Anna hurt. Before very long I shall either put a stop to these clandestine meetings between you or make them public knowledge. So you had better make up your mind which it is to be," she scolded.

Chad nodded his head in agreement and mumbled to the effect that he had been thinking about it. Then, anxious to change the subject and knowing through Anna where Caroline's interest lay, he said, "Pierce will be there—I'll make sure of that, I promise."

"Thank you." Caroline did her best to sound indifferent. "But I am far more concerned that little Anna should be included in the invitation. If she isn't, then you may tell your mother that I regret I shall have a previous engagement on that day."

"But I haven't told you which day it is," Chad spluttered.

"That makes no difference. Whichever day it is, I'm perfectly sure that both my aunt and I will be unable to attend."

Chad's slow mind suddenly grasped the meaning behind Caroline's words. "You really are determined to force my hand, aren't you, Lady Caroline?"

"Yes," Caroline replied unwaveringly. "It's high time you acted like a man instead of pussyfooting around." As she spoke, Caroline recalled Pierce Chinery's words the night of the assembly at Fort York. 'A gentleman would have dreamed of doing it, but only a man would have done it.' She was quite certain that Pierce wouldn't need any prompting, were he in similar circumstances. Knowing how much Chad admired him, she said this, and Chad agreed.

"But it's different for him," the young man bleated. "Pierce is used to working with his hands. I'm not. If I cross my parents, my father will cut off my allowance and I won't get the appointment he has arranged for me in the legislature."

Caroline took one of Chad's hands in her own and inspected it. Her own pretty ones were less white than they had been on arrival, and bore signs of manual work. "They look a perfectly normal pair of hands to me, Chad. I see no reason why they couldn't learn to hew wood and till soil just as well as anyone's. There's no shame in honest toil."

"Hypocrite!" her aunt said after Chad had taken his leave of them. She had been sitting in a corner of the veranda mending the boys' pants—an endless job, it seemed. "You know, my dear, listening to you just then, I could almost hear Captain Chinery speaking. You really will have to make up your mind whose side of the fence you are on, Caroline, or you will become dizzy running around in circles."

Caroline chose to ignore the implication. "Well, don't you agree about Anna, Aunt Eliza?"

"Of course I do. You know perfectly well what my feelings are in that respect. I was referring to your own, niece."

"I have no particular feelings as far as Pierce Chinery is concerned," Caroline replied with a toss of her head. Then she went indoors to help Mary set the table.

Anna was so excited that the Kendalls had actually sent her an invitation to one of their very select gatherings that she made a special journey into town to tell Caroline before going to Monsieur Quetton St. George's store to purchase some sprigged muslin for a new gown.

"I'm determined to look my best, if I have to sit up every night sewing. I must do nothing to let you down, for I know that I owe it all to you, my dear friend."

"Nonsense!" Lady Caroline replied. "Come upstairs, I want to look in my closet. I have a feeling that my new pink gown will suit you to perfection. No one has seen it, for I have come to realize that with my colour hair it is quite the wrong shade." Actually she looked very well in it, but she was determined that Anna should be as well dressed as anyone at the picnic.

For the first time in weeks there were storm clouds over the lake on the morning of the Kendalls' party. "I hope it's not an omen," Stephen Fairchild remarked over breakfast.

"Why should it be?" his sister asked as she wiped the stickiness from little Ben's face. Both she and Caroline had become quite adept at caring for the children, although Caroline frequently threatened the boys with immediate extinction in a most unladylike manner. On their part, they had quite taken to their pretty cousin and enjoyed teasing her no end.

"Because, though I am not usually given to imaginings," her brother replied, "I have an unhappy feeling that the mix today may well prove explosive, especially with you two there to light the fuse."

"Fiddlesdediddle!" Eliza retorted. "In such a select society, I'm sure we shall all act with perfect docorum."

"We shall have little opportunity to do anything else," Caroline chimed in. "Whenever any of the Kendalls are about, other than Chad, everyone becomes frozen with anxiety, for as a family, I vow, I have never met any so conscious of position. One may scarcely lift a cup to his lips before Mrs. Kendall deemed it permissible. Anyone would think that she was born to the purple."

"Well, you know what they say about putting a beggar on horseback. Of course she keeps very dark about her antecedents, but I have heard that her grandfather was a blacksmith somewhere in the Midlands of England," Stephen replied.

"This is certainly a land of opportunity in more ways than one," Eliza Fairchild remarked. "It offers all the riffraff from the Old Country the chance to come over here and pass themselves off as gentry, when back home they would be fortunate to obtain a position as a parlour maid."

The two Fairchild ladies were plainly in a belligerent humour as far as the Kendalls were concerned, and Stephen had grave misgivings as to the outcome of the day's events, as well he might.

The Kendalls' country estate encompassed several thousand acres of some of the most fertile land in the area, naturally. It reached right down to the shoreline on either side of the river to the west of the town; for that reason it was easier for them to travel by water along the edge of the lake. The journey would have been exceedingly pleasant and soothing had it not been for the fact that Colonel Rowlands was in their canoe. Nevertheless, Caroline found the soft sound of the paddle less obtrusive than the splash of oars would have been.

She sat trailing her hand in the cool water and looking up at the green banks with their clusters of elm, basswood, and butternut trees giving a softer line to the landscape than the dark pines on the hills beyond. An eagle soared high overhead, and along the riverbanks a variety of small creatures, most of them, like the beaver, quite unfamiliar to her, scurried about their business. Here and there a willow dipped its delicate green fronds into the flowing waters.

As she started the climb up the banks toward the picnic site, Caroline wondered if Pierce Chinery would be there. Chad had not mentioned whether he had accepted the invitation, and she would not ask. Oliver Rowlands grasped her arm and guided her steps in a most proprietary manner, refusing to let go, although she insisted that she could manage perfectly well on her own. He seemed to think that the casual exchanges of conversation that they had indulged in recently gave him the right to control her every move.

"I do wish that Colonel Rowlands would keep his hands to himself," she had said to her aunt while they were dressing that morning. "But of late he takes every opportunity to touch me, and his hands send shivers up and down my spine."

Eliza Fairchild's eyes narrowed as she listened; she too had noticed that the colonel's advances were becoming more intimate, even though Caroline did her best to avoid them. However, he appeared to be a gentleman, and she hoped she could rely on his instincts to behave as one, but she had every intention of keeping a close watch on him that day.

A marquee had been erected in which a military band was playing, and wooden benches had been dotted around under the trees. No expense had been spared, and while Mrs. Kendall sat in a large basket chair, which Caroline likened to Cleopatra on her golden throne, her guests were at liberty to wander about the hillside or down to the river at their leisure.

Anna and her uncle had chosen to come overland and were already there by the time the Fairchilds arrived. Caroline, having paid her respects to her host and hostess, walked amongst the guests hoping to catch a glimpse of Pierce, but it was nearly time for luncheon before she caught sight of the big black stallion and recognized the tall broad-shouldered figure of the captain. He was looking exceedingly handsome in a dark green tailcoat, white breeches, and riding boots of fine black leather. His appearance caused quite a flutter amongst the little group of young ladies as he approached.

"Mercy on us, wonders will never cease!" one of them remarked. "I do declare that Pierce Chinery is becoming quite the fashion plate since your arrival, Lady Caroline. Before that it was hard enough to get him to attend our little gatherings, let alone take such trouble over his appearance."

Oliver Rowlands, who had hardly left her side, moved in a little closer. "Possibly, ma'am. But I would remind you that clothes cannot make a man a gentleman if he doesn't have the makings in him."

"How very true," Caroline murmured, moving forward lest Pierce should be put off by the colonel's proximity. She had long regretted her spat with him and hoped that today would offer the opportunity to make amends. Pierce came across and greeted them all. As he bent to kiss her hand, their eyes met and for a fleeting moment there was a glimmer of his old smile. Caroline increased the pressure of her fingers and prayed that he would understand she wanted to be friends again.

Luncheon was served, and the wine and ale, specially imported for the occasion, flowed freely. By the end of the meal several of the young bloods showed distinct signs of having imbibed too freely. Eliza Fairchild remarked to Caroline that she considered Oliver Rowlands was more than a little tipsy and she should be on her guard.

While the tables were being cleared away and the ground prepared for the entertainment and dancing that were to follow, Caroline wandered down toward the river with Anna. The poor girl was beginning to feel quite depressed, because Chad had paid scarce attention to her the whole morning. Caroline did not comment, but she knew that he was afraid to appear too friendly in front of his family, and she hoped that when she led Anna away from the throng toward a small copse that lay in their path, he might take the hint and join them, which he did.

Caroline left the two lovebirds to wander deeper into the cover of the woods and began the return journey, thinking all the while of Pierce. She heard the crunch of footsteps on the dry underbrush and looked up, hoping that it might be he, but her expression changed as she saw the tall figure of Oliver Rowlands coming toward her.

"I missed you," he said, coming up and taking her arm. "You know it's not safe for anyone as lovely as you to go wandering about alone like this." His speech was slurred, and there was a strong odour of drink upon his breath. Caroline did her best to move away, but he held her closer to his side.

"The time has passed for pretty party games, Caroline," he rasped, gripping her wrist and swinging her around to face him. "You and I were meant for each other; there is no one else of our kind in this wretched wilderness, and I need a mate." His hand closed about her throat, bringing her face close to his. "It will be my pleasure to teach you what love is all about before or after marriage—either way is of no account." As his thin lips pressed down upon her mouth, stifling her cry, Caroline caught the sadistic gleam in his dark eyes.

Panic seized her, and she fought like a tiger. With her

one free hand she tore at his face until he was forced to breathe. But the more she struggled, the tighter he held her, tearing her gown as she attempted to pull away. For the moment her mouth was free, and she called out, hoping that Chad would hear and come to her rescue. Then the pressure of Rowlands' arms forced the breath from her body, and she spun down into darkness.

It was some seconds before she began to recover her senses, to find herself lying on the ground, her head in Anna's lap. Her friend was bathing her brow with water Chad had fetched from the river in his tall hat. Slowly Caroline began to recall what had happened, and then her attention was caught by angry sounds accompanied by heavy breathing and the thud of blows. With Anna's help she managed to sit up, and a few yards away in a small clearing she saw Pierce Chinery and Oliver Rowlands fighting like a pair of angry lions.

The two were well matched for size, and both knew how to use their fists, but neither was paying particular attention to the gentlemanly art of fisticuffs. Giving blow for blow, their fury increasing all the while, they dodged about skillfully, avoiding the tree stumps that lay in their path.

The sound of the commotion had attracted the attention of the other guests, and they had begun to congregate around the two men, some of the younger ones calling encouragement to the contestants, depending upon whom they favoured.

Eliza Fairchild rushed to help Caroline, and she and Anna assisted her to her feet. "For pity's sake, aunt, make them stop fighting or they will kill each other," Caroline implored. But it was useless, for neither man would listen to the command of John Kendall or the pleas of Stephen Fairchild and the count. Their rage blinded them and forced even their supporters to fall silent. Their clothes torn and dirty and their faces begrimed from the many falls they were taking, they battled on, but slowly it became obvious that Rowlands was tiring; he was befuddled by drink and his physical condition did not match his opponent's. Finally, with a heavy blow to the jaw, Pierce felled him, and Rowlands lay dazed upon the ground.

Chinery stood there panting, waiting for him to regain his feet, but the colonel had had enough. He staggered up and lurched away out of range, but Pierce grabbed him by what was left of his coat. "Now, you apologize and grovel like the vermin you are," he said, lifting the colonel bodily and carrying him over to where Caroline was standing propped against a tree.

"Damn you, Chinery," Rowlands growled, flinging himself free from the other's grasp and turning to go; but his way was barred by Chad, his fair young face flushed with shame and anger.

"Do as Pierce says, cousin, or you will have to answer to me."

Rowlands gave a strangled laugh and attempted to push Chad away. When Chad refused to move, he tried to force his way past. "Get out of my way, you young whippersnapper . . . you and your dollymop over there," he shouted, gesticulating toward Anna.

A gasp of horror went up from the onlookers; even the ladies recognized the term men applied to the whores that frequented the taverns in the town.

"I'll kill you for that," Chad screamed, diving at his cousin. "I'll have you know that lady is to be my wife."

"Great Jehoshaphat!" Eliza Fairchild exclaimed. "Now we have an angry bull to add to the circus."

But John Kendall had reached his son's side and laid a restraining hand upon his arm. Chad's sudden announcement had a sobering effect upon Rowlands, and bowing contemptuously first to Caroline and then Anna, he turned and staggered off down toward the canoes on the river.

Mrs. Kendall collapsed into hysterics and had to be assisted back to the house, while the rest of the party, shocked by all that had happened, began to disperse; no one felt in the mood to continue the party. John Kendall apologized abjectly to Stephen Fairchild, who, Eliza told Caroline, was angrier than she had ever known him to be.

Pierce, having recovered from his effort, came across to where Caroline was standing trembling like a leaf in the wind. Without saying a word, he swept her up in his arms and started down toward the river, calling over his shoulder to Chad to see that his horse got back home safely because he was taking the Fairchilds back.

The whole affair was the sole topic of conversation in the entire community for the next few days. Caroline was so embarrassed that she refused to leave her room, although Eliza and Anna, who came to see how she was the following day, both assured her that no one held her in any way responsible for what had taken place. There had already been a minor scandal concerning the colonel and a young housemaid, so his reputation was far from being untarnished.

But Caroline was not thinking so much about the rest of society, she was wondering how Pierce Chinery felt about it all. Eliza said he was probably at home nursing his bruises. "He may have won in the end," she said. "But he certainly took some punishment before he put the colonel down for good."

"Whatever Pierce may be suffering, I guarantee Rowlands has worse," Stephen remarked with a great measure of satisfaction. He had come up to see how his niece was feeling. "Although I am angry at the reason for it, I must admit it was a mighty fine fight. I haven't seen anything like it since I was a young man and used to go down to Brighton or out to Finsbury to see Gentleman Joe or Belper in the ring."

Eliza Fairchild sniffed disapprovingly. "I sincerely hope you are not likening this to a common prizefight. Captain Chinery was defending your niece's honour."

"I'm well aware of that, Eliza. I only wish that I had been a few years younger so that I might have pitched in there myself. It was a most disgusting affair, and I don't see how Rowlands will ever have the gall to show his face in polite society again. As for the Kendalls, it has been a most rude setback for them. They say Mrs. Kendall is quite overwrought and has taken to her bed, refusing to speak to anyone."

Caroline was beginning to recover from her shock, and the many messages of sympathy she had received proved a balm to her injured pride. She was therefore prepared to turn her attention to other matters. "And what has happened about Chad's announcement of his intention to marry Anna? She made no mention of it when she came to see me, and I did not think it advisable to ask at that moment."

"I think everyone was too stunned to take it in at the time, but I met Chad in town this morning. He was on his way over to see the count and make a formal proposal. I was quite struck by the change that has come over him. Under their present burden of disgrace, John Kendall apparently decided it was unwise to provoke social opinion by opposing the match. He has given it his blessing, and even agreed to try to improve the count's property by giving Chad several hundred acres adjoining it for a wedding present. No doubt he hopes to reestablish himself with us all by appearing benevolent."

"It's a little late for that," Eliza said. "But I'm happy for the count's sake . . . and of course for Anna," she added hastily as she noticed the amused smirk on Caroline's face.

Anna came bustling in the following day full of excitement over her news. Chad had spoken to her uncle, who had readily given his consent, and now her head was giddy with plans for her wedding. She presented Caroline with a beautiful bouquet of garden flowers, but it was some minutes later before she remembered to mention that it was Pierce who sent them. He had ridden over to see them that morning with the express desire that Anna should bring his gift to Caroline. He said he was in no fit state to be seen at the moment, but would call and pay his respects in a day or so.

"Has he suffered much injury?" Caroline asked anxiously.

Anna giggled rather unsympathetically for her. "Well, let us just say that he is not quite as handsome as usual. But apart from a cut lip and a black eye, he seems little the worse, and I've no doubt he will be as good-looking as ever in a short while."

Caroline nestled her face in the flowers. She felt better now that she had heard from Pierce. She had been so afraid lest he should hold her partly responsible for Rowlands' behaviour. His gift had lifted her spirits so much that she agreed to accompany Anna downstairs to consult Miss Fairchild over the arrangements for the wedding.

Remembering the shabbiness of their little homestead, Eliza Fairchild was quick to suggest that as there was no other lady at home to assist the count, they might like to hold the wedding from Stephen's house. "It is so much nearer the church, and it would save you and your uncle a good deal of travelling seeing to all the arrangements."

Etienne de la Fayre, who had accompanied his niece and was talking to Stephen, was more than happy to agree. The poor man looked quite wan from all the excitement, and was relieved to hand everything over into Eliza's capable hands. Before Anna left that evening, the date was set for the middle of September, and Caroline and Prissy were to be bridesmaids.

"I suppose I should ask Blanche, as she is to be my sister-in-law," Anna said a little ruefully.

"I think you had better," Eliza agreed. "I have a feeling that for some time she will be much more disposed to be amiable to everyone."

"Don't worry," Caroline laughed. "At the first sign of any disagreeable behaviour from her, I shall murmur 'Oliver Rowlands.' That will quickly change her tune."

From that day on, the Fairchild household was turned upside down. Hannah and Mrs. Ryan were as excited as anyone at having a wedding in the family, for so they thought of it. The house had to be cleaned from top to bottom, and on most evenings Stephen went off to the garrison to play cards. He said the officers' mess was the only place he could get away from cackling females.

It was more than ten days after the incident at the picnic before Pierce Chinery was willing to show his face in town. Caroline opened the door to him, her eyes shining with pleasure, although she had to smile, for his face still showed the remnants of the battle.

"Do I still look so bad?" he inquired as he followed her to a secluded corner of the veranda.

"They are honourable scars," she said. "Please don't think I was laughing at you, for I shall be eternally grateful for what you did."

"I wouldn't blame you for laughing. You should have seen me the day afterward. My only consolation was that Rowlands must have looked a sight worse, and I fancy it will take him a while longer to recover."

"He has far more than physical wounds to recover from."

"Aye, that's for sure." Pierce sounded grim. "But from all accounts, you will not need to trouble your pretty head about him again. I hear that John Kendall has ordered him out of town, and before the end of the week he will be on his way back to England."

"That will be very pleasant for him," Caroline remarked, making a mental note to write and inform some of her friends about the nature of the man in case their paths should cross.

"But enough of him," Pierce said, sipping the tea that Mary had brought out to them. "I fancy this calls for a celebration, for did you not say that you were determined to see Chad and Anna married? While I do not commend the way it happened, you undoubtedly supplied the means which brought it about. I was in despair of ever finding a way to make Chad speak up for what he wanted."

Caroline gave a shy smile as she looked across at him. "That is not one of your failings, I'm happy to say, Pierce."

The grey eyes gazed back at her unwaveringly, and the expression in them made her heart skip a beat. She was suddenly afraid of what he might be going to say, and what she would answer if he did. "The trouble is," she said falteringly, "we don't always know what we want, do we?"

"I suppose not." Her companion became unusually quiet and contented himself with finishing off his tea. When he had finished, he said, "I suppose you will be making plans to go back home after the wedding? You will not want to spend the winter out here."

"I can't . . . I mean, I have . . ." Caroline blurted out, and then tried to cover her tracks. "I mean that it is my intention to stay until next spring."

Pierce looked at her quizzically. "Really? I would have thought you'd wish to escape the bleakness of a Canadian winter. Don't tell me that the bright life of the city is losing some of its attraction for you?"

Caroline longed to tell him the truth about her wager with D'Arcy Letton, but for some reason she felt that he would not approve of her taking the subject of matrimony so lightly. "Let us just say that between you and Anna, I'm beginning to discover some of the magic you both feel out here, and I want to see what the winter holds in store for me." She laughed.

"Do you mean that?" he asked seriously. "Or are you just putting me on?"

"Putting you on—what a quaint way you have of expressing yourself, Pierce. If you mean, was I teasing you—the answer is no. I'm beginning to understand the country and the people a little better, and I don't feel quite so lonely as I did at first."

"Good! But you will find that we have a number of quaint ways about us, and not all of them may be to your liking. However, you might as well find out about one of the better habits we have in these parts. I'm having a barn-raising party shortly, and I wondered if you and Miss Eliza would care to come. Chad and Anna have already agreed. Mind you, this is not a society affair. Some of the more radical members of the set will be there, but many would consider it beneath them."

Caroline felt slighted by his last remark. "And you think that I might be one of them?"

"No, I didn't mean that," Pierce hastened to reply. "I

now know you well enough to realize that you are not a snob in that sense."

"Thank you," Caroline retorted wryly. "But you still consider that I am in many others?"

"I didn't say so." Pierce laughed. "So don't get up on your high horse again. Have you always been so prickly, or is it merely the heat out here?"

"You once told me that you thought we were two of a kind, you and I, so perhaps you should look to yourself when it comes to being prickly," Caroline countered merrily. She was determined not to be provoked into an argument with Pierce again. The last one had led her into trouble. If she hadn't wanted to annoy him, she would never have encouraged Oliver Rowlands.

"I guess you're right," Pierce said, getting up to leave. "But I've never met such a gal for making a man's hackles rise. You're like an unbroken colt—I can never tell what you may be going to do next."

"Well, don't try breaking me in," she said, "or you will be in for a nasty tumble."

"I'll risk the fall," he said, raising her hands to his lips. "But I'd sure hate to see anyone break your spirit."

9

Eliza Fairchild reluctantly declined to attend the barn raising that Pierce had arranged for the Logans, saying that she was too busy with the preparations for Anna's wedding. Caroline had a sneaking feeling that her aunt didn't want to miss Etienne de la Fayre, whose visits were becoming increasingly more frequent. However, Miss Fairchild said she saw no reason why Caroline shouldn't go, as Anna and many of their other acquaintances would be there. Necessity was quickly schooling them both to be less inhibited about going unchaperoned, although the "Rowlands affair" had left Eliza nervous for her niece's safety.

True to his word, Pierce had given the Logans sufficient

land to start a small farm of their own. Caroline had heard him telling her uncle that they were to pay for it in kind, by continuing to help him with the house and farm. She recalled that Pierce had said he would do this when he was ready to set up housekeeping for himself, and she wondered miserably when that was to happen.

Chad Kendall called for her, and together they rode out along Yonge Street to meet Anna. On the way, they were joined by an odd assortment of vehicles, all headed in the same direction. Caroline was amazed to find that they were actually making for Pierce Chinery's farm.

"Great Jehoshaphat!" she exclaimed. "What is he going to do with all these women and children?" for there were entire families piled into wagons or on horseback.

"Oh, there'll be plenty for everyone to do, you wait and see. The men and boys will be busy with the barn, while the ladies keep us well nourished with food and drink. Then, when it's finished tonight, we shall all have a party."

"You mean that you intend to finish building it in one day?" Caroline said incredulously.

"We sure are. Harvest is almost upon us, so there is no time to spare. That's why we are all throwing in our lot to help the Logans. You know what they say: 'Many hands make light work.' "

Caroline was amused to notice the manly approach Chad was taking to the project. It was only a short time ago that he had been whimpering about being unable to work with his hands. However, now that he was to be married and become a man of property himself, he had suddenly developed a grave air of responsibility. It had taken the episode with Rowlands for him to find his manhood, but having done so, he plainly had no intention of turning back.

Even though it was quite early, the sun was high in the sky and Caroline was thankful for the pretty cotton sunbonnet Hannah had made for her. Anna had warned her not to wear anything too grand for the occasion, so acting on her advice, Caroline had on a simple cotton gown sprigged with tiny flowers. Her aunt had laughed when she had seen her. "My dear, you look as pretty as a picture, but what would they say at Walford House if you appeared in that garb?"

"I can't imagine," Caroline rejoined. "But as I'm unlikely to be invited to a barn raising in Hyde Park, that is something I'm never likely to encounter."

"You are still set upon returning to England when the

year is up?" Eliza did not wish to influence her niece unduly, but already she knew that she was going to miss her if she went home.

Caroline shook her head merrily, for she was in a holiday mood. "Don't ask me that now, aunt. I don't know what I want to do, and I'm afraid to think about it. I seem to have made so many mistakes in the past."

"The only serious mistake you ever made was entering upon that wager with Letton. But even that may turn out to be for the best in the end; sometimes our mistakes can turn out to be blessings in disguise."

Pierce was equally complimentary about her appearance when he came to help her dismount. "Well, now," he said, holding her waist in his two hands just a little longer than necessary, "you sure have changed, Lady Caroline. I could easily mistake you for a country gal—and a mighty pretty one, at that."

"I'd remind you of your own thoughts on that point," she replied, blushing becomingly. "Clothes don't make the man or the woman. Just because I look countrified won't stop me from being a city girl at heart."

"True," Pierce said, depositing her safely on the ground. "But like the missionaries, I shall try to convert the heathen."

By the time they had all assembled, there were at least fifty men and their families, not counting those that popped in to give an hour or two of their time now and again. Mrs. Logan and several of the other women had obviously spent days preparing a magnificent spread, which they had set out on sawhorse tables under the trees. Pierce had provided plenty of liquid refreshment—lemonade or tea for the ladies, and whiskey for the men. As he told Caroline, barn raising was mighty thirsty work.

He was to be the captain, and the men divided into two teams to add more fun and excitement to the job, for each side was determined to beat the other to the finish. Caroline and Anna spent their time helping to serve refreshments and playing with the younger children. Sometimes Caroline just sat under the trees and watched the huge brilliantly coloured butterflies fluttering amidst the flowers or hovering over the ripening wheat.

Pierce was busy directing the workers, so could spend little time with her, except during the lunch break. He came and sat down under the tree by her side, and they both made a hearty meal of meat pies, ham, sausages, fruit pies, and cake.

"It is just as well that I don't do this kind of thing too often, or there wouldn't be a gown in my wardrobe that would fit me."

"You've a way to go before you need worry about that," Pierce said, casting a glance over the slim figure sitting against the tree beside him. "There's no flesh on you. If I were to take you to market, I'd be lucky to get a wooden nickel for you." He laughed, but he was noticing how thin she had grown in recent weeks. He paused to finish off a slice of pie before saying rather more seriously, "This isn't your kind of life, though, is it? You would much rather have an elegant table with silver and fine linen, wouldn't you?"

Caroline refused to be drawn. "You really enjoy this life, don't you? You don't have to answer that, for I can see it in the way you work. And it's quite obvious that the people have a great respect for your abilities. Perhaps you should do as Chad suggests and enter politics. You feel so strongly about their rights, and they need someone with your education to speak up for them."

"I've thought about it," Pierce replied. "But I'd be running against the tide as far as most of the principal people are concerned. There are a number of them now only too ready to label me a republican Yankee who only wants to upset the establishment here."

"But you're not, are you?"

"No, that's why I came to Canada. I'm not a radical, but there are many things that need changing—things that were good when this country started, but we are a progressing people, and institutions need to grow with the times." He paused to brush away a mosquito that was trying to settle on her neck. Then, cupping her chin in his hand, he looked down into her eyes. "This place is growing so rapidly, in a few years it will match up with the cities in the East; that's why I think you should stay here, Caroline. Oh, I know it will be a long while before it catches up with London in size, and our ways will never be the same; they can't be, because our life is so different. But it could be a good life."

Caroline turned her head away. Once again she had the feeling that he was about to say something she was not ready to hear because she didn't know the answer. "I'm sure it will be, especially if you are willing to help lead them to the promised land," she said flippantly.

Pierce let a sigh escape him as he said, "That ain't as easy as it sounds, ma'am. It's lonesome enough at times without deliberately cutting myself off from a lot of people I now think of as friends."

"You don't have to," Caroline replied. "You can set about converting those heathens, just as you are trying to do with me."

Pierce laughed and jumped to his feet, ready to resume work. "I haven't the same incentive. They're not nearly such attractive heathens, Carrie." She watched him stride over to join the rest of the workers preparing for the roof raising. She was such a stranger to this world, and he was so much a part if it.

Anna called her attention to a small group of Ojibways standing back in the deep shade of the surrounding forest. Pierce apparently knew them, because he called out to the men to come and join in the fun. They moved forward slowly, waiting to make sure they were welcome. One or two of the settlers didn't look too happy, but there was no open hostility, and it was soon forgotten in the general laughter and horseplay that lightened their toil.

Caroline picked up a basket of fruit and took it across to the women and children. They smiled shyly, the little ones hiding behind their mothers' skirts. As she turned to leave them, she was conscious of a tension in the air, and one of the women grabbed her by the arm. Caroline started to draw back in fear until she realized that the woman was not concerned with her. The Indian stood poised and tense, straining all her senses to recognize something away in the distance. Whatever it was she sensed was suddenly confirmed. She said something in her native tongue that caused the others to turn and flee, while she rushed past Caroline, calling attention to something that was happening deep in the forest.

A hush quickly fell over the workers, and they too stood listening for a second before they scattered, some to climb trees, others to various vantage points from where they could scan the horizon. Pierce, who had run to the top of a nearby rise, called urgently, "It's due north and heading for the Paynes' farm unless the wind shifts."

The whole place was suddenly in an uproar. The men, grabbing whatever tools they could lay their hands on, jumped onto horses and into the wagons, regardless of who they belonged to. No one stopped to question what had to be done. The women were already searching for fallen branches and anything else that could be used as weapons against the oncoming fire.

Panic seized Caroline as she stood there feeling helpless. Anna came rushing past armed with a garden hoe and a wooden spade. "What shall I do?" Caroline asked, ashamed to be the only one standing still.

"You can come with us or stay with the older women and help move the children out if it gets too close."

"I'd rather come with you," Caroline said, scrambling into the wagon beside her friend. "Do you think they'll be able to stop it? What do you do when something like this happens?"

"Pray for rain," Anna replied, scanning the sky in the direction of the lake. "And dig ditches to try to divert its path."

Long before they were near enough to feel the heat from the fire, Caroline caught sight of the flames leaping high above the tall pines. The forest was like tinder after the summer sun. Her heart started to beat wildly as she heard the crackle of falling branches and the cracking of trees.

They soon came to a small stream where a man blocked their path, saying they could go no farther and that they should start a trench that side of the water. On the far side a chain of men was passing buckets to others, who used the water to dampen the underbrush as a breaker against the all-consuming flames.

Caroline took the spade from Anna and started digging and scratching at the baked earth. Her back aching, she paused for a second to look down on the small log cabin in the dip below. A crowd of people had gone to help the family pile their belongings onto the wagon that had been drawn up outside, while on the far ridge the first tongues of fire licked at the trees.

"It could rain," one of the women said, cheering them on. "Let's pray to the good Lord that it does." Caroline heard some of them begin to murmur under their breath, and she joined in silently as she went back to her digging, dreading to think of what the consequences might be if their prayers went unanswered.

But the miracle happened. In the distance there was the long low growl of thunder. Caroline usually dreaded the fierce, unexpected storms that often swept across the lake, but today she welcomed it with a sense of relief and thanksgiving.

Within a short time it was overhead, and the clouds broke, dowsing the countryside in torrential rain. A great cry of joy went up from everyone around, and many, their arms uplifted, ignored the downpour and danced until they looked like drowned rats. The rest of them found what shelter they could and waited to make sure the fire had abated. Then, dirty and wet, they all trooped back to the barn raising, intent on finishing the job they had set out to do.

After some much-needed refreshment, the men set to work again with renewed vigour, knowing that now time was against them if they were to complete the building that night. The stars were already twinkling in the clear night sky long before the last timber was in place, but somehow it was done, and after some further refreshment, most of it liquid, two of the group brought out their fiddles and the party began. Everyone was tired and dirty but ridiculously happy; they had fought a battle against time and the elements and they had won.

Caroline had done her best to clean herself up, but her gown was beyond repair and her hands sore and blistered from her valiant efforts with the spade. Pierce, stripped to the waist, had taken his place in the queue of men dunking their heads and arms in the large wooden laundry tubs, washing off the worst of the sweat and grime. The light from lanterns hanging from the tree branches shone on the water as it slithered over his muscular back and chest. Then, shaking the surplus from his curly head, he pulled on his old shirt, tucking it in as he came toward her laughing.

"That was quite a day!" he said, taking her hand. Then, noticing her wince, he turned it over. He raised it to his lips and kissed her wounds. "I truly meant it when I said I wouldn't like to see them after they had been using an ax, but you can be mighty proud of those scars, ma'am." Then he led her forth to join the first dance.

"You're mad . . . you're all quite mad." Caroline joined in his laughter, but there was a note in her voice that suggested she meant what she was saying. "How can you bear to live under these conditions?"

"Listen," Pierce whispered in her ear, "they're playing our tune." He started to sing. "There was a wee farmer who lived in this town . . . And he tore up the ground, the devil knows how . . ."

"Only a fool or a devil would or could do it," Caroline said bluntly.

"Yes . . . I suppose you're right, Lady Caroline," he replied ruefully.

The music quickly changed, and Anna and Chad joined them for a round dance. The party continued until long into the night, which was now warm and beautifully clear. Caroline was relieved to think that she had arranged to spend the night with Anna, for her aunt would have had fifty blue fits if she had arrived home in the middle of the night in her present state. She couldn't even begin to imagine what Miss Fairchild would say to the way she was cavorting with the local inhabitants, regardless of social degree. And had she known that her niece walked back through the forest hand in hand with Pierce Chinery, with a harvest moon shining down from a velvety blue sky, or that when he said good night he drew her tenderly into his arms and kissed her, Miss Eliza Fairchild would most surely have had conniptions. But Caroline did all those things, and what is more, she enjoyed them.

The next few weeks were so busy that scarcely anyone had time to call his own. It seemed to Caroline that everyone was caught up in some form of harvesting, the men with the crops and the women gathering the wild berries that grew so plentifully in the countryside. The growing season in Canada was much shorter than back home, and it was not unknown for the frost to strike the crops by late August, which could prove devastating to a community which had of necessity to be as self-sufficient as possible. And after the fruit was gathered, it had to be washed and turned into preserves, while the grain was being threshed and winnowed for the winter store.

Miss Fairchild had written the invitations for Chad and Anna's wedding in her delicate pointed handwriting, and her two nephews along with Sean Ryan had been dispatched to deliver them far and wide. Even the society ladies quite forgot any animosity they might have felt toward Anna, now that she was to become a Kendall, and found time to hold regular sewing bees to help her prepare her trousseau. Some of them had made her a handsome quilt of many colours, and on one occasion they wove as much as sixty yards of lines at one bee. The settlers' wives from quite distant parts of the district arrived almost daily, bringing items that they had made for the household. Caroline could not help but be impressed by the way they all contributed so willingly to the bride's new home.

There was also an undercurrent of excitement in the Fairchild household on their own account. Since Oliver Rowlands had left the province, his house on Front Street was now vacant, and Stephen decided that his growing family could well use the extra room it afforded. Caroline was given the task of planning the refurnishing and accompanied her uncle to an auction of the colonel's household effects to advise him on the pieces he should purchase. Such a sale was a great event in their lives, and nearly everyone of any account was there, including Pierce. Much to Caroline's chagrin, he outbid them on a number of articles to which he knew she was particularly inclined.

They planned to move in before the winter, and in turn this affected Count de la Fayre. Having no longer to worry about Anna's future, he could now use what little money he had for his own purposes. He confided to Miss Fairchild, and she heartily agreed with him, that he thought Chad and Anna should be left on their own at the start of their married life. With Chad's money they were already making plans to improve the little log house. Etienne therefore decided to take Mr. Fairchild up on his offer and rent their present residence on King Street. All in all, there was soon to be a general change-about. However, this was not to take place until the young couple were married and away on their honeymoon. Anna had never been outside the province, so Chad had arranged a tour that would take them to Montreal and down the eastern border to New York, stopping with Pierce Chinery's parents on the way.

Caroline spent most of her time, when she wasn't attending a bee of one kind or another, tidying up the garden. She had won Henry to her side earlier in the year and he had dug over the long-neglected flowerbeds in which he had planted the seeds and cuttings she had begged from Pierce and other friends. Now she set a hired man to scythe the grass on the back lot in preparation for the marquee they were borrowing from the garrison for the wedding reception.

Her garden had flourished, and as she knelt amongst the brightly coloured blooms—roses, larkspur, lilies, and the deep gold of the yellow nymphaea—listening to the raucous cry of the creasted blue jay perched on a branch above her head, Caroline felt at peace with the world. She was far too busy to be bored, as she had so often been back home. And on the rare occasions when she had nothing in particular to fill her thoughts, she could always think of Pierce. In fact, quite often when she should have been concentrating on other, more pressing things, she found herself thinking of him. Like everyone else, he was too busy for regular visiting, but he never came into town without stopping by to pay his respects and inquire how the preparations were progressing.

He had agreed to "stand up" for Chad at the wedding, which had not pleased the Kendalls, as they would have preferred a member of their own family to be the best man. But, as Caroline said, Chad took courage from Pierce and would feel stronger if he were by his side. The Kendalls had given way with as much grace as they could muster. They were still feeling under a cloud socially since the disgraceful behaviour of Colonel Rowlands and were hoping that the wedding would efface the memory of that incident from people's minds.

On this particular morning Pierce had come along the back lane of the Fairchild property, and seeing Caroline busy weeding her flowers, he quickly jumped the low white picket fence.

"You can come and do some of that for me when you've finished here," he joked. "For I have scant time for anything but harvesting at the moment."

Miss Eliza came out of the house and joined them just then. Having overheard Pierce's remark, she said, "You should find yourself a wife, Captain Chinery."

"Aye, ma'am, I've been giving that question quite some thought lately."

"We have enough work on our hands preparing for Anna's marriage," Caroline remarked abruptly. "So I should put any thought of it out of your mind until we have seen them safely wed."

"Yes, of course." Pierce sounded abashed, and Miss Fairchild frowned at her niece disapprovingly.

Captain Chinery soon took his leave of them after promising to let Caroline have some of his best roses for the bridal bouquet. As soon as he had gone, Eliza spoke her mind, as was her wont. "What do you think you are doing, niece? Is it your intention to drive that young man away? Because if it is, then you are about to make yet another mistake. For if ever I have seen two people in love with each other, it is you and Pierce Chinery."

"If you think that, aunt," Caroline said, gathering up her gardening tools, "then you know more than I do about the workings of my heart. I'm not saying that I am not attracted to him, but to admit to anything more is out of the question. Apart from any other reason, you know as well as I do that I am not free to consider the possibility of marriage until after the period of my wager. I'll never have it said that Caroline Fairchild failed to honour a gambling debt."

Her aunt sighed. "If you only knew how many sleepless hours I have spent worrying about that foolish wager. I can't begin to tell you what anxiety it causes me to think of you being forced into a marriage with D'Arcy Letton."

"It wouldn't be the first time such a marriage had come about. It is said that my Lady Hamilton was won at a gaming table," Caroline replied with a touch of irony her aunt was quick to note.

"I hope that you are not comparing yourself with her?" Eliza retorted angrily. "She was another man's mistress at the time, and he put her up as the stake in a game of cards. The situation is bad enough as it is, but at least you still have your honour." Miss Fairchild refrained from mentioning that she had just received a letter from England, saying that Letton had disappeared, having recently killed yet another man in a duel. It was rumoured that the reason had been a woman, but whatever the cause, the news was most disturbing.

Caroline tried to lighten her aunt's gloomy mood by saying, "Yes, at least you can be thankful for that. Although if Colonel Rowlands had had his way, I doubt if I should be able to say that. But never fear, I've not the slightest intention of letting Sir D'Arcy win. I've discovered that I still have quite a lot of growing up to do. I've wasted far too much of my life in idle nonsense, and I do not mean to tie myself to a man who thinks of little else, nor let him have my money to indulge his whims."

"I'm beginning to think that you might do a lot worse than marry Pierce Chinery," Eliza said. "Oh, I know he does not have the rank, and if you were ever to return home, it would prove embarrassing. But I too have learned a great many things since coming here. By the majority of people, rank is viewed very differently, and I'm not at all sure they are not right. Captain Chinery is far more of a gentleman than D'Arcy Letton could ever hope to be."

"Oh, I must tell Pierce that he has won a convert." Caroline laughed. "Coming from you, Aunt Eliza, that's almost seditious. I shall have to watch, or you'll be joining the ranks of those republicans who think that Canada should join the States."

"Never!" Her aunt was shocked at the suggestion. "You know perfectly well that I have always supported the monarchy. But that does not mean to say I always agree with some of the things that the government and society decree. There is a great deal of injustice both in England and out here. And I've come to the conclusion that in many ways it is far worse in the old country. At least out here there is a chance that the more liberally minded men like Chinery will be able to set things straight before too much power gets into the hands of the wrong people."

"Yes," her niece replied. "I think that perhaps you're right. As the Yankees say, 'we are a progressing people.' "

At that moment Mrs. Ryan came out to say Miss Blanche Kendall was waiting on them with regard to some of the wedding arrangements. Caroline heaved a sigh of resignation. Circumstances were forcing her into a closer acquaintanceship with Blanche than was her intention. For to know Blanche Kendall better was to know only too well that the first impression of the wretched girl was more than justified. However, Caroline was determined that nothing should mar Anna's wedding day. So, composing her features into something resembling a smile of welcome, she accompanied her aunt into the house to discuss the final plans for the following week's great event.

Caroline was up and about early on the morning of the wedding, as was everyone else in the household. It was her self-appointed task to make sure that Anna was the prettiest bride in Christendom. It was so fortunate that the count was of Huguenot stock and they could have a church wedding, because as yet there was no Catholic church—nor any other denomination, for that matter. Those who were inclined all worshipped at St. James's, regardless of their faith, but weddings and christenings often had to be delayed for a visiting priest or Methodist preacher.

First she attended to little Prissy, who was full of excitement at wearing her new white muslin gown for the first time. Then Caroline put on her own blue Indian silk gown with its delicate white lace fichu and set out her poke bonnet and elbow-length mittens to be collected at the last moment. After that she devoted the rest of her time to Anna.

It was a hot sunny day, with seagulls swirling high above them in a cloudless sky as the procession left for the church in open carriages. It seemed as if all the citizens of York and many from the surrounding countryside had come out to see the bride. Anna was very popular, and many of them called out, wishing her well.

"Happy the bride the sun shines on," Caroline said, thinking how different King Street looked from the first day she had driven along it. The little front yards behind the white picket fences had sprung to life, and sunflowers, lupins, daisies, and hollyhocks nodded at them as they passed, while the bell in its cradle beside the little wooden church (as yet there was no steeple) pealed out a welcome to the bride and her guests.

It was true the procession was made up of an odd assortment of carriages. John Kendall had lent the count and Anna his stylish new phaeton; Caroline, Blanche, and Prissy preceded them in the Fairchilds' calèche, with Henry up front. Miss Eliza, the boys, and Stephen Fairchild, who was holding the reins, went ahead in the coach. And before them went all manner of vehicles, from gaudily painted coaches that were little more than farm wagons in disguise, to plain carts drawn by oxen straight from the fields, although they had been groomed and decorated for the occasion.

"I can't think why Anna insisted on inviting such people," Blanche said, viewing the motley collection with a cold critical eye.

"They've been good friends," Caroline rushed to their defense.

"Goodness is not always a sufficent quality to qualify one for acceptance in society," Blanch sniffed. "I sincerely hope that Anna will change her ways after her marriage. But from what I have seen, she does not appear to realize the honour that is being done her today."

"If it means turning her back upon old friends, then I hope she never does," Caroline snapped back. She had an insane urge to push her companion out onto the road and go ahead without her. But little Prissy was watching them with large questioning eyes.

"Speaking of old friends, there is quite a surprise in store for you, Lady Caroline," Blanche said, curling her lip in a rather curious smile.

Caroline did not take in the full import of Blanche's remark, for they had just arrived at the church, and having alighted, it was their task to attend to the bride. Besides, Caroline was anxious to try to catch a glimpse of Pierce. The church was quite small, and she could see him standing head and shoulders above the others near the altar. Both he and

Chad looked very smart, although the bridegroom's face was as pale as white-pine bark.

The church was crowded to capacity with the families of the socially elite group whom the Kendalls counted their friends. And even though they had invitations, many of Anna's and the count's guests were forced to stand outside. Caroline heard rumblings of discontent from some of the younger men, although they were quick to doff their hats and shout their compliments to the bride.

As the small procession moved down the aisle, Pierce turned to look at her and their eyes met. For one ridiculous moment Caroline wished that she were the bride and he the groom, but then her attention was caught up in the proceedings. It wasn't until they turned to leave that she discovered the meaning of Miss Kendall's earlier remark, for Caroline suddenly found herself staring into the dark brooding eyes of D'Arcy Letton.

The shock was so great that for a moment she thought she was going to faint. Fortunuately Miss Fairchild was sitting close at hand, and she managed to catch her niece's eye and frown a warning to her. But how she managed to complete the journey back to the house, Caroline would never know. She was so thankful that convention demanded that Pierce should be her escort for the day—a duty he was more than willing to fulfill.

Chad was busy passing around tiny pieces of cake wrapped in white paper, which, having been passed through the bride's ring, were by tradition supposed to cause the unmarried ladies present to dream of their future husbands.

"I shall be very interested to know the outcome of your dreams tonight," Pierce said as he watched Caroline take her packet.

"I have a fancy that it will be more in the nature of a nightmare," she said unthinkingly, her eyes on D'Arcy Letton.

"Yes, I imagine this little shindig is vastly different from the fashionable weddings that you are used to attending, Lady Caroline."

But Caroline was not paying attention to what he said, and he followed the line of her gaze. "Do you know Sir D'Arcy Letton, the Kendalls' cousin?" Pierce asked. Before he could get a reply, Letton had come across to greet them.

"My dear Lady Caroline," he said, bowing and kissing her hand. "How very good it is to see you again. I must say that you are looking remarkably well, for which I am glad.

As you know, I had the gravest misgivings about your survival in this wilderness."

Caroline felt Pierce stiffen at Sir D'Arcy's tone, and she hastened to introduce them, hoping to change the subject, but the captain had no intention of letting it pass unnoticed.

"I take it that you're another one like Lady Caroline, who finds the ways of the colonials rather quaint, Sir D'Arcy?" There was a bitter sting to his voice that she had never neard before, even when they had been sparring.

Letton had already eyed Chinery's elegant attire and mistakenly took him for one of the snobbish elite. "Well, my dear fellow, I'm sure you are of a mind with me: no one in his senses would choose to live in such a backwood. Let us admit between ourselves that we are here to make as much money as we can before speeding back to civilization. Of course, it may be different for you. Blanche tells me that you're a Yankee." His tone was vaguely insulting, and again Caroline sensed that Pierce was bristling.

Anxious to prevent the antagonism between them deepening, she took D'Arcy by the arm. "Come and pay your respects to my aunt," Caroline said, almost dragging him away.

"I've already spoken to the good lady," Letton replied. "But as you know, I'm always ready to follow wherever you may care to lead, my dear Caroline." His manner was unnecessarily familiar, and she shuddered to think what effect it was having on Pierce.

The rest of the day was ruined for Caroline, although she did her best not to let Anna be aware of anyting wrong. Pierce hardly came near her, and when he did, he was overly polite. She saw Blanche talking to him on more than one occasion, and would have given the world to have known what Miss Kendall was saying.

Anna and Chad were not due to leave for their honeymoon trip for another day or so, and when the young couple were ready to retire, the peace of the evening was broken by the strident sounds of a shivaree. Most of the guests had already departed, only a few of their friends remaining behind to help clear up after the feast. As the cacophony of tin plates, cow bells, drums, and any other things capable of making an infernal din broke upon the night air, Caroline almost jumped out of her skin. She turned, thankful to find Pierce standing close beside her.

"Don't worry," he said rather caustically. "It's just another wild colonial custom." He pointed to a crowd of young rakes gathered beneath the window of the bridal chamber. It was impossible to see their faces, as they wore corn masks and other disguises; but they were yelling and whooping it up with alarming ferocity.

"How long will they keep it up?" she asked.

"All night, if they've a mind to. But if they let off some of their steam, I may be able to bribe them away with the promise of more liquor and another party at one of the taverns. But I'd advise you not to let them see your disapproval. They are in their cups, and they will not take it kindly. It's a good job they are well disposed toward Chad and Anna, for if they disapprove of a match, I've seen these affairs turn ugly."

"Disapprove?" Caroline queried. "What business is it of theirs?"

"None, by rights," Pierce was quick to agree. "But having little out here in the way of law and order, everyone tends to make his own rules of behaviour. And if many of them feel a match is unsuitable, as when an old man marries a younger woman, or sometimes for hidden political motives, the shivaree becomes an excuse to cause a riot."

Caroline gave a slight shiver at the thought. "What's the matter?" Pierce laughed. "Does it remind you of the wolves howling?"

"Given my choice, I would prefer the wolves," Caroline replied. "I see little fun in this except for those taking part."

"Your admirer Sir D'Arcy is one of them. He's out there with a number of the Kendall clan."

"That doesn't altogether surprise me. D'Arcy always had a taste for the bizarre."

"Really, you quite amaze me, Lady Caroline. Your tone sounds as though you don't altogether approve of Letton."

"I don't. It is merely that he was one of the set back home."

"Again you surprise me. From what Miss Kendall said, I imagined that he was rather more than an acquaintance, or why else should you have promised him your hand in marriage?" Pierce said coldly, his eyes the colour of granite.

"Is that what Blanche told you?" Caroline gasped.

"Can you deny it?"

The tears brimmed up into Caroline's amber eyes. "I told

you that I once made a foolish wager. It was with Letton, and my hand was the stake against his fortune."

"Were you so desperate for money, Lady Caroline, or was it a way to capture Sir D'Arcy Letton's heart? I cannot think it was for the title, although Blanche did mention that he was heir to Lord Letton. In spite of the fact that you find rank so important, your own already exceeds his expectations."

"You are extremely well informed on the rank and file of the British aristocracy, Pierce." Caroline tried to cover the misery she was feeling by sounding flippant and unconcerned. "But I did not do it for love or money, and as you rightly say, I already outrank him. I did it because he provoked me. It was a moment's madness." There was much more that she would have liked to say to Pierce, but it might appear as though she were begging for his understanding, or worse still, his love. She was far too proud to do that.

"I see," Captain Chinery said quietly. "It would seem that there is a far greater gulf between us than I thought. Out here we may be rough-and-ready people, but we do not take our relationships lightly, especially when it comes to matrimony. We do not consider it a sport to wager on." He gave an abrupt bow and went out to quieten the noisy revellers. Caroline fled upstairs to the sanctuary of her room, where she flung herself down on the bed and sobbed.

10

If it were possible, the ensuing weeks were even more hectic than when they had been preparing for the wedding. With Chad and Anna away, Count de la Fayre had no one on whom he could depend to help him with his move into town. The other settlers were frantically finishing the harvest, and by September they had started the fall plowing.

Anna had begged him to delay the move until their return, but the count rightly thought that the newlyweds should have the farm to themselves on their return. Miss Fairchild told her niece that he also wanted them to stay away from the Kendalls' influence until Anna had become used to being mistress in her own home.

Of course, before the count's move could take place, the Fairchilds had to remove themselves to Colonel Rowlands' old home. Furtunately this did not take too long, as Stephen was able to muster the necessary help, and Caroline was pleased to find Pierce was amongst them.

She had not seen or heard of him since the wedding, while D'Arcy Letton had been in almost constant attendance. Caroline had been grateful for the excuse of moving house, as it meant she didn't have to spend any more time than necessary in his company. The only thing that made his visits at all bearable was that Blanche Kendall always accompanied him whenever she could find an excuse to do so. With Anna out of the way, she had been quick to claim Caroline's friendship, and she had let it be known publicly that they were bosom companions. Caroline had had no part in it, but she did not contradict the gossip, as it gave her a reason to encourage Miss Kendall to come with Letton. Her aunt said she detected an increasing air of jealousy on Blanche's part over the attention D'Arcy insisted on paying the Fairchilds—Caroline in particular.

"Oh, she can have him, aunt, with my most sincere gratitude, if she would only take him off my hands."

Eliza was worried because her niece showed marked signs of going into a decline. She rarely laughed and had little of her old fire and energy, although she insisted on doing her part in helping to get them settled in their new home. Miss Fairchild hoped that the sight of Pierce Chinery would help to bring her out of her melancholy humour, but the two barely exchanged greetings and the captain left as soon as the last piece of furniture had been set in place.

The last weeks of September brought the rains, refreshing after the long hot summer but turning the roads into a mire. Consequently Etienne de la Fayre wisely decided to delay his move until such time as it cleared. Everyone assured Caroline that the dismal rains would not last long, and then they would have an Indian summer before the winter snows.

Caroline sat at the window of her bedroom looking out over the harbour. The new house being much larger, she was able to have the place all to herself, which she found gratifying. Fond as she was of her aunt, she had always been used to her own quarters, and in her present mood she found her aunt's continual inquiries as to her state of health tended to fray her nerves.

The docks were busy with vessels of all kinds coming and going with passengers and cargo. Stephen Fairchild told them they always tried to clear as much by water during late September and early October, because after that it was anybody's guess how soon the lakes would become treacherous and impassable because of ice. The grey skies and the sad cry of the loons out on the lake matched Caroline's mood as she thought of the onset of winter. D'Arcy Letton never missed a chance of reminding her how long and bleak she would find it, and Caroline became more and more certain that his main purpose in coming to York Town was to make her life so wretched that she would give up and go home before the year was over. Although no one had spoken of it openly, Caroline knew that the news of their wager was all over town. She had overheard her young cousin Mark telling his brother that many of the young bloods at school were placing side bets on which one would win. There was still no doubt in Caroline's mind that she would see it through to the end, but now that Pierce had almost disappeared from her life, she was finding it very bitter indeed.

Her reverie was broken by a knock at the door, and Miss Fairchild came in. "How are you feeling, my dear?"

"Oh, for pity's sake, don't keep asking me that question," her niece snapped back irritably. "I've told you already there is absolutely nothing wrong with me . . . nothing that going back to England won't cure."

"You don't believe that, Caroline, any more than I do. You'll have no peace of mind, my dear, until you decide what you want from life."

"That is a lot easier said than done. . . . And even if I knew, it may not be in my power to achieve it." Caroline was already sorry for the way she had spoken to her aunt, who only had her niece's welfare at heart.

"That's true," Eliza Fairchild agreed. "And in your case, it is hard, because you have always been in a position to have nearly everything you've ever desired. But if it will make you feel any better, I am faced with a similar problem."

Caroline looked up quickly. Ever since the time in London when Miss Fairchild had confessed the story of her own lost dreams, Caroline had tried to be more attentive about other people's aspirations. "What is it, aunt? There's nothing wrong, I hope?"

Eliza Fairchild looked flushed and a trifle embarrassed. "No, there's nothing wrong, but I felt that I needed someone to talk to, and I didn't want to mention it to Stephen until I had made up my mind. There is no sense in disturbing him if I should decide against it."

Caroline had to laugh in spite of her grey mood. Normally her aunt was a very levelheaded person, but today she wasn't making much sense. "It would help a great deal if you were to tell me what you are talking about."

"Yes, of course," Eliza replied. She came across and sat in the armchair facing Caroline, but her thoughts were obviously miles away. She gazed out at the grey waters of the lake for some minutes before she spoke again, and Caroline did not like to break the silence, for her aunt was plainly disturbed. Eventually Miss Fairchild looked up, intent on seeing her niece's reaction to what she was about to say.

"Etienne de la Fayre has asked me to be his wife," she said bluntly.

"Why, that's wonderful," Caroline responded, smiling with relief, for she had been anticipating something far more shocking.

"Do you really mean that?" Her aunt gave a sigh. "I have been so worried in case you should disapprove or think I was deserting you in any way."

"What utter nonsense," Caroline replied vehemently, remembering all the lonely years her aunt had spent caring for other people. "It is more than time that you looked to your own happiness, and I think it will be a perfectly splendid match. I hope you agreed?"

"I told him that I would think about it. There are so many other things involved. I came out here to look after Stephen and the children."

"And there is absolutely no reason why you shouldn't continue to do so. You will be living almost next door, and Hannah is already devoted to them. Let her continue here, and we shall look around for someone to help you. For that matter, Mrs. Ryan would probably be very pleased to be your housekeeper. It is far too extravagant keeping two such excellent cooks in one household. We will find another young girl to assist Mary, and don't forget that I will be around to help for a while yet."

"You make it all sound so easy," her aunt said gratefully. "But I'm also concerned about your future. If you go back to England, who is going to look after you?"

"D'Arcy Letton, if I don't win the wager!" Caroline laughed. "But seriously, aunt, you must look to yourself over this. You have waited quite long enough to become mistress of your own house, and I for one will make sure that it comes about." She got up and put her arms about Eliza, kissing her gently on the brow.

"Thank you, my dear. I must say that is a great relief, for you were the one person I was most concerned about. I will be quite near if Stephen should need me, and he has plenty of friends. As it is, he spends most of his evenings playing cards up at the garrison. I've often thought I should be very lonely if you were to go home."

"Now, you are not to concern yourself with me. I've learned a great many things over the past few months, and I promise you I'll never do anything so foolish again. As for Uncle Stephen, I'm sure he will be more than happy for you. He has the highest regard for the count. Anyway, who knows, there is always the chance he may wish to marry again himself. I've heard him complimenting Hannah on being such a good cook and caring so well for the children."

Her aunt laughed at the suggestion, then stopped and said in a serious tone, "Of course, that is not nearly so improbable as it sounds over here. But I cannot imagine what the Duke of Walford would say if his brother were to marry the cook."

Caroline was going to say that the idea was quite ridiculous, but she stopped suddenly, questioning her own reasons for saying so. Not long ago she had accused her aunt of becoming a convert to Pierce Chinery's radical philosophy. Now it would seem that she was in danger of doing the same thing herself. For there was no valid reason why Hannah couldn't make an admirable wife for her uncle, should he so desire it. "Fortunately we do not have to worry about what the duke might say, as the matter has not arisen as yet," she said in reply to her aunt's remark. "But let us return to your news. If you return the counts affections—as it is obvious to me that you do—then you must put the poor man out of his misery at the first possible moment. When do you plan to marry?"

"Good heavens, my dear, I haven't even given it a

thought," her aunt replied, remedying the omission almost immediately. "It couldn't possibly be before Christmas. We must give Anna and Chad a chance to settle in first, and then I would like to feel a little more certain about your plans before committing myself to a date."

"Well, if you won't do it, then I shall have to take over and make all the arrangements for you as you did for Anna." Caroline was quite pleased at the prospect of having something to occupy her thoughts in the weeks to come. "I suggest that we have it early in the new year, then you will be able to go away for a few weeks before I return to England. That way you will have a light heart knowing that Uncle Stephen and the children have my undivided attention."

Her aunt gave a slight grimace. "It won't be undivided if D'Arcy Letton has his way. That man is becoming a pest. Having discovered that he is making little or no headway with you, he has started paying court to me, no doubt hoping to win me to his side. He so aggravated me the other day when I was in Mr. de Quetton's store that I walked out, saying I would return when it was less crowded."

"I know, Blanche Kendall came and told me. She was very upset because everyone in there had noticed the snub, and she sincerely hoped they didn't think it was directed at her as well as Letton." Caroline was quite amused at the thought of the flutter the little scene had caused. But at the same time she was conscious of a slight shudder of fear down her spine. Letton was known for his quick temper and excessive pride; he was not a man to forget an injury, real or imagined.

By the end of the second week in October the rains had cleared and the sun was hot enough to quickly dry out the ground, still hard from its summer baking. Caroline arose on the first clear morning and looked out of her window. The sight that met her eyes caused her to catch her breath, for a transformation appeared to have taken place. The leaves had begun to turn before the wet weather set in, and since then she had paid them scant attention, thinking they would fall much as they did back home. Beautiful as the autumn could be in England, it could never hope to surpass the Canadian fall. The maple leaves, shaded from brilliant red through rose pink to gold, fluttered in the breeze, while walnut, beech, and many others added a variety of amber, yellow, and gold to the scene. And when the sun caught them, they seemed to burn with a life and vitality that made a lie of the dying year. Here, if ever, there was a promise of rebirth and renewal. It seemed as if nature was intent on leaving a message of hope to help them through the long winter that lay ahead.

Having little else to do, Caroline decided to ride out to Etienne de la Fayre's place and help him with the preparations for his move. They had had a small party a few evenings earlier to celebrate his betrothal to Miss Fairchild, and Caroline had promised at the time that she would visit as soon as the weather had cleared.

Her uncle warned her to wrap up, saying that the sun soon lost its strength at this season and he already detected frost in the air. Unfortunately, Caroline paid little heed to the warning, and thinking that she would probably be too hot in her green velvet riding habit, she refused to take a cloak with her in spite of her aunt's protestations.

It was a decision that she soon regretted when she entered the sheltered depths of the forest. Amidst the trees the sun's energy was turned into brilliant shafts of light, and its warmth was lost. Caroline shivered as she allowed the little mare to pick its own way over ruts in the dirt road. The puddles from the recent rains had soon dried out, but the constant traffic of wagons passing to and fro had left it uneven and difficult to travel. She could understand now why Stephen Fairchild said that it would be easier when the snow was on the ground; once it had frozen hard, the surface would be smooth and she could use the sleigh.

Caroline had passed several travellers along the way, but by the time she reached the forest, passersby were few and far between. Those having business in the town had set out early in the morning and were not yet ready to return. Consequently she had the road to herself—or so it appeared. Once again she was caught up in the mystery and majesty of the forest, as she had been on the night of the garrison assembly.

At first it seemed so still and quiet except for her horse's hooves upon the road, but as she listened, she became aware of myriad sounds. Small creatures scurried unseen through the underbrush, while squirrels chattered and swung precariously from the tree branches over her head, busy preparing their winter stores. She heard a strange hoarse bark, and looking up between the tall pines, Caroline watched a flock of wild geese flying south to avoid the coming snows. These, and the glowing colours of the grasses and leaves caught in the pale sunlight, wove a tapestry of sight and sound it would not be easy to forget.

Once again she found herself comparing it to the hustle and bustle of Knightsbridge on a sunny morning, or the carriages bouncing briskly around the crescent past Walford House. She imagined herself promenading in St. James's or Kensington Gardens, acknowledging the unstinted admiration of all who passed her by. There she reigned supreme in a world she understood and over which she appeared to have control. Here she had been subjected to violence and brutality, but she had also discovered a warmth and kindness lacking in the fashionable London salons. The trouble was, Caroline no longer knew to which world she wanted to belong.

She had come to a small clearing where a miniature waterfall cascaded down over the rocks, the clear water sparkling like diamonds on the sunlight. She dismounted and sat on a fallen tree to ponder her future, enjoying the warmth after the crisp cool air of the woods.

She had been sitting there for only a few minutes when she heard the sound of a rider approaching from the direction in which she was headed. She watched to see if it was anyone she knew. The population was still so small that she was quickly becoming acquainted with many of the settlers, if only by sight; many of them she had met at the barn raising. But her heart skipped a beat as she recognized the big black stallion belonging to Pierce Chinery. She stood up and moved forward to attract his attention, afraid that he would pass her by, he appeared so deep in thought.

"Good morning, Pierce," she greeted him, wondering if he would stop or merely return her salutation before continuing on his way.

But he looked up with some surprise and smiled as he saw her standing in a shaft of light that turned her amber hair to a deep rich gold. "Why, Caroline, the spirits of the wood must have overheard my thoughts. I was just on my way to see you and pay my respects to Miss Fairchild. I have already stopped to offer my congratulations to Count de la Fayre."

"My aunt was very sorry you were unable to come to the small dinner party we gave to mark their betrothal," Caroline said, recalling how wretched she had felt when she had seen his letter regretfully refusing the invitation.

"Yes, I too was sorry not to be able to attend, but it has been a very busy time at the farm, and I have been making preparations to go away for several weeks."

"Oh!" she exclaimed, and had difficulty not to show her disappointment and shock at hearing the news.

"Yes," Pierce continued, dismounting and slipping the reins of his horse over a branch next to her little bay mare. "I have to go to Boston on business. It may even necessitate my going to England. A great deal will depend on my father."

"He's not ill, I trust," Caroline said anxiously, but at the same time hoping Pierce would tell her more of his reasons.

"Oh, no, he's in excellent health, thank you. It is only that the business is complex, and I'm not sure that it will be altogether pleasing to him, so I may have to undertake it myself."

"Will you be gone long?" she asked. Then added quickly, "We shall all miss you," lest he should mistakenly think her distress at the news was in any way personal.

"I wonder," he replied, and it was obvious from his manner that he was thinking only of her. "It is said that absence makes the heart grow fonder . . . but I think it is more likely to forget, don't you?"

"It depends on your memories." Caroline turned away and tried to concentrate on the water splashing along its merry way. "Some people find it easier to forget than others do."

"And what about you?" Pierce said, taking one of her hands in both his strong brown ones. "You can't forget, can you? I can still see it in your eyes. This will never be home for you—your heart is thousands of miles away in England. Unless . . ." He paused, and she turned back to look at him. "Unless," he continued with a wicked grin, "you have given it to Sir D'Arcy since his arrival here?"

A spark of the old fire returned to Caroline. "That isn't fair. I thought I had made it quite clear how I felt about that relationship." She recalled his tone of disgust when she had told him the truth about the wager. A few weeks ago she would have been too proud and considered it none of his business, but now, especially as he was going away, she wanted so badly for him to understand. "It was a very stupid thing I did, and I admit it. But I was much younger then, although it was only a few months ago. I realize now that growing up is not a matter of time, it is a matter of experience. And I've had plenty of new experiences since coming out here."

Pierce gave a slight laugh, but his tone was suddenly apprehensive as he said, "My word, there has been a change. Is this the same young lady who threatened to have me whipped for taking such liberties with her when I carried her off the boat? I can hardly believe my ears, she was so sure that her world was the right one. What has happened to that old spark of fire that used to flame up whenever I made you angry?"

"I'm not sure of anything anymore, Pierce. I no longer seem to have the same spirit of 'do or dare' I once had," she replied sadly.

"That won't do," he said tersely, taking her face in his hands and looking down into the depths of her amber eyes. "If you are to survive and win out here, then you must be ready to face the devil and come back again to fight some more. Whatever happens, you mustn't let it break your spirit."

"I won't," she said, but it was not very convincing, and the tears brimmed up into her eyes. Tenderly he drew her into the circle of his arms and kissed her gently on the lips. She laid her head against his chest and fought desperately to stop herself from sobbing.

"What?" he said laughingly as he released her. "No fireworks . . . no slap across the wrist . . . no struggle? Why, matters must be much worse that I thought if I can't raise the merest flicker of anger in those fiery eyes of yours."

Missing the warmth of his arms, Caroline shivered more from misery than cold, although she suddenly felt an alarming chill run through her.

With a look of concern, Pierce quickly slipped out of the cloak he was wearing and wrapped it around her. "Come," he said. "I'm going to take you home to your aunt and get her to dose you with some whiskey and wild-cherry bark, for you could well be sickening from an attack of fever."

"I was on my way to see if I could help the count with his preparations to move," Caroline protested after making a face at the mention of the proposed treatment.

"I'll call on my way home and explain the circumstances." Pierce sounded as though he would brook no argument even if she were in the mood to battle. He picked her up and swung her into the saddle.

"I can manage," Caroline said. "There is no call for you to see me home if you are busy with your preparations."

"I've finished now," Pierce replied, jumping up onto his horse alongside her. "I was on my way to make my farewells, for I leave tomorrow. But you will soon have Anna and Chad back amongst you, and before you know it, it will be spring."

"I hope so," Caroline said forlornly. "But just at the moment, spring seems an eternity away."

When they arrived back at the house on Front Street, Miss Fairchild was most upset to hear Pierce say he thought Caroline was sickening with fever, although it only served to confirm her own suspicions. She packed her niece off to bed and refused to listen to any excuses. Her instructions were backed up wholeheartedly by Pierce, and Caroline felt far too weary to fight them both.

The first snow had already fallen, and Christmas was nearly upon them before Caroline was fit to be up and about again. True to their predictions, she had succumbed to a severe attack of fever and had barely recovered from its initial attack when it struck again. For several days her life itself hung in the balance. The doctor put it down to her already debilitated condition. However, Miss Fairchild had other ideas as to the cause. She blamed herself for foolishly allowing Blanche Kendall to visit Caroline while she was still convalescing, and after the wretched girl had left, she went upstairs to find her niece in tears.

"My dear, what on earth is the matter?" She hastened to get Caroline back into bed. She had been sitting by the window watching the snow that had been falling unceasingly since early morning.

"It's nothing . . . just weakness . . ." Caroline sobbed. This was true to a degree, but her aunt knew her too well not to realize there was more behind it.

"It's that wretched Kendall girl. I must have taken leave of my senses to have allowed her to come up to see you, but I was attending to little Prissy, who has developed a nasty cold, and I had agreed before I realized it. What did she say to upset you so much?" Aunt Eliza's eyes were blazing.

"Oh, she was just repeating some gossip that she had heard."

"Regarding Pierce Chinery, no doubt?" her aunt made an educated guess. Caroline nodded as she sipped down the vile-tasting medication with which her aunt kept dosing her. "Well, I can tell you that he is perfectly well. Your uncle had a letter from him this morning in which he says that he will be remaining in Boston over Christmas but hopes to see us early in the new year. I was going to bring it up to show you later. He especially inquires after your health."

"That was only common courtesy," Caroline sniffed. "He could do little else. But Blanche has heard through a mutual friend that he has gone to find himself a wife. . . . Apparently his father has a cousin in England who has a daughter who spent several months with the Chinerys. And it was with her family he stayed when visiting London." She burst into a fresh flood of tears. "So . . . no doubt . . . it is she whom he will bring back here as his bride."

"He makes no mention of it in his letter," Miss Fairchild said. "And I certainly wouldn't give it any credence until I heard it from Pierce himself." She plumped up the pillows and put a cool hand upon her niece's brow. She was anxious not to let the conversation continue along the same lines, for she had heard the same rumour herself while out shopping that morning. "Mercy's sake, Caroline, you must stop this crying at once or I shall have to send for the doctor, for your head is as hot as a burning coal."

That had been early in November, and now Anna was busy decorating the invalid's room with evergreens. "The doctor tells us that if you continue to improve, you will be able to come down and have Christmas dinner with us all," she said brightly. She had returned from her honeymoon all aglow and had just confided in Caroline that before the next year was over there would be another Kendall in the community. Caroline had been delighted at the news, only remarking that if it was a girl she sincerely hoped they wouldn't name her Blanche. "We have already decided that it will be Helene, after my mother. Helene Eliza Caroline Kendall."

"It will probably be a boy," Caroline said gloomily, contemplating the stark landscape outside. "But no matter, just as long as he is strong and healthy."

"You poor dear," Anna said, fussing over her and tucking her round with an extra shawl. "You have been shut away up here far too long, you're not a bit like your usual self. I was only saying to Chad how much I miss you around. You add such a sparkle to our lives, you know."

"Thank you," Caroline replied, "but I will soon be down. I have no intention of waiting until Christmas. I intend to see my aunt and your uncle married in the new year, and then I will be returning to England."

The news had a shattering effect upon poor Anna, for she like everyone else was well aware of what that would mean. "Oh, no, you can't mean that. At least wait until the spring," Anna cried.

"You mean until the period of the wager is over. I've been giving that a lot of thought while I have been lying up here alone, and I've come to the conclusion that it would be better to marry D'Arcy than die an old maid. At least I shall have children to comfort me. And I've not the least doubt, knowing him, that as soon as he has his hands on my money, I shall see very little of him, for he will spend day and night at the gaming tables. But do not mention any of this abroad, as I intend to keep him in suspense as long as possible."

"I've not only no intention of mentioning it, I've no intention of letting you do it if I can find a way to prevent you," Anna retorted indignantly. "I know now what a happy marriage can mean for a woman, and I can't bear to think of you tied to that man for the rest of your days. You are only saying this because you feel low and depressed after the fever. You'll soon cheer up when Pierce returns. He can always make you laugh, even when he's making you mad."

"Yes, I must get well so I can dance at his wedding." There was such bitterness in Caroline's voice that Anna put down the string of coloured beads with which she had been decorating the evergreens, there being no bright red holly in Canada.

"What makes you say that?" she asked, coming to sit opposite Caroline. "Has Blanche Kendall been gossipping?"

Caroline told her what Blanche had said some weeks ago about Pierce going in search of a wife, and Anna looked quite vexed. "Blanche is the one dark spot on my happiness. Even Mrs. Kendall has become quite tolerable in her manner toward me, but my sister-in-law grows more spiteful every day."

"No doubt she is jealous of your happiness, for she must be past the marriageable age. In England she would already have been banished to a remote corner to concentrate on her crochet. I can almost find it in my heart to feel sorry for her," Caroline said, thinking of her aunt in similar circumstances. "That is why I have decided that marriage to Letton is better than remaining a spinster for the rest of my days."

"What nonsense," Anna declaimed hotly. "Why, she is years older than you. Blanche must be twenty-five if she is a day, although she is most secretive about her age. But as to this business about Pierce, it is nothing more than idle gossip. I'm sure Chad would have been one of the first to know if there had been anyone to whom Pierce was attached other than yourself."

Caroline brightened up a little. "How do you know he felt any more for me than friendship demands?"

"I'm not even going to answer that, for you know the answer yourself."

Caroline had the grace to blush, but said, "I know we always seemed to end up arguing, which is no recommendation for a happy partnership. He once said he thought we were two of a kind." She paused, remembering the sweet wild moments in their relationship.

"That is not necessarily a bad thing, provided there is a mutual love that binds you together. You know you would both get heartily bored with the placid life that suits Chad and me. And if Pierce should to into politics, as rumour is rife that he will, you would make him a splendid helpmate. He would need your strength and courage to support him."

Caroline laughed ironically. "My strength, did you say? Why, just at the moment I doubt if I could kill a fly."

"You wait until the sun returns. Your strength will come with it. So let us have no more talk of your marrying Sir D'Arcy, for I will not allow it. Neither will Pierce—of that I'm sure."

Anna's words had cheered her no end, and in spite of her aunt and the doctor's protestations, Caroline insisted on coming downstairs a full week before Christmas so that she could supervise preparations for Miss Fairchild's wedding. They had agreed that it would be a very quiet affair. The service was to be held in the front parlour of the house, and only a few close friends were to be invited.

"At my advanced age," Miss Eliza said, "I do not think it seemly to make a great deal of fuss. The news has already caused enough stir in the town as it is."

Something in her aunt's tone made Caroline look up from her task of dipping the long wick in a cauldron of mutton fat for the extra supply of Christmas candles. She was sitting in front of a blazing fire in the big kitchen, and Hannah had wrapped her round with a pile of shawls to make sure she didn't take cold again.

"I cannot see that it has anything to do with the rest of the population, but why do you say it has caused a stir?"

Hannah and Mrs. Ryan were both upstairs cleaning, and

Miss Fairchild was sorting the clean linen. She did not reply immediately, but waited until she had put a pile of tablecloths away in the drawer of the big wooden dresser. Even then she did not give a direct answer. "You don't think I'm a foolish old woman venturing on such a partnership at my time of life, do you, Caroline?"

"Of course not. I've never heard anything so absurd. Who has dared to suggest such a thing?" Caroline's cheeks were burning, but this time it was anger, not fever, that made them so red.

"Oh, it was just something I heard young Mark telling Joseph the other day."

"What has that terror been up to this time? He has a sight too much to say for himself on occasions, if you ask me." Caroline recalled his remarks regarding her wager with Letton.

Her aunt sighed. "It's foolish of me to be concerned about a pack of boys, but apparently the Kendalls were making some ribald comments upon the subject. Actually, Mark apparently tried to defend me; there was a fight, and he received a whipping for his pains."

"Good for Mark. I'm glad he's inherited some of the Fairchild spirit. I must remember to give him a large box of candy."

Her aunt smiled with relief to hear Caroline show some of her old fire. She came across and removed the rack of freshly dipped candles out of Caroline's reach. "I'm pleased to find you are recovering some of your spirit, for that has worried me more than anything else. But you have done more than sufficient work for one day. I'm not risking the chance of a relapse. I want you well and bonny for my wedding day. Besides, you must be fighting fit before Pierce Chinery returns."

Caroline looked up quickly. "Why? Have you had some news of him?" She wondered if her aunt was thinking she would need all her strength to face up to the news he would bring with him.

"Your uncle received a letter this morning saying that he would be home in time to attend the wedding and asking after your health."

"Was that all he had to say?"

"Yes. Apart from asking for some instructions to be passed along to Ryan about the farm. Why? Were you expecting something more?"

"I wondered if he had mentioned anything about England . . . and I thought he might have written to me," Caroline said plaintively.

"He knows you have been ill. He probably had no wish to write, as it would mean you would be put to the trouble of answering him. Anyway, you have so often behaved like a prickly pear whenever he's around, that you can hardly blame him for being cautious in his approach."

Miss Fairchild's remark made Caroline throw back her head and rock with laughter, much to her aunt's surprise, as it was such a change from a moment ago. She raised her eyebrows in a manner which called upon her niece to explain.

"I'm sorry, aunt," Caroline said between laughs. "But caution is not one of Pierce Chinery's traits. If he wants something badly enough, then he is the type of man to go right out after it, of that I'm sure." She fell silent for a second or so, then said in a quieter tone, "No, if Pierce held any deeper feelings for me than he has already displayed, he would not hesitate to say so. But he will always love this country and his land more than he will ever love a woman, and as I have no mind to play second fiddle in any man's affections, I have already resolved that nothing more will come of that relationship."

There was a note of lingering regret in Caroline's voice that caused Miss Eliza to come across and put her hand on her niece's shoulder with a sigh. She knew from the set of Caroline's jaw that it was useless to pursue the matter further. "Oh, dear! I'm afraid that with you two it will always be a case of flint striking steel—there will always be a spark."

Caroline reached up and patted her hand. "Then don't fret yourself about it, aunt. It is all for the best, for if we were to mate, between us we might well set the world on fire."

Mrs. Ryan came in at that moment to say Sir D'Arcy had called to inquire when Lady Caroline would be well enough to receive visitors and to leave a packet of tea and a large box of candies.

"Never, so far as he's concerned," Miss Fairchild said testily.

"Please convey my thanks and tell him that I hope to be well enough to receive early next week," Caroline said. After Mrs. Ryan had gone, she turned to her aunt. "Really, Aunt Eliza, I thought I was supposed to be the firebrand in this family. Don't you think it would be wiser to modify your approach to Sir D'Arcy? This is a small community, and even after Letton returns to England, you will have to live with the Kendalls." She did not add that her aunt might also have to become reconciled to having Letton as her nephew, if only by marriage.

Her aunt gave a little snort of disgust. "After a letter I received from your uncle in London regarding Sir D'Arcy's finances, I have a most ominous feeling that he may never return and we shall have to live out the rest of our lives with him in our midst. I wish to heaven he would marry Blanche Kendall. She has more than enough for both of them, and that way we should be rid of two of the most obnoxious people it has ever been my misfortune to know."

It was Caroline's turn to raise her brows in surprise. "What do you mean when you say that Sir D'Arcy is having money troubles? Upon my word, I sincerely hope not. If you remember, it was his fortune against my hand in marriage. Don't tell me he won't be able to honour his debt after all I've been through to win."

"It wouldn't be the first time he had defaulted. The duke tells me that Letton has been blackballed from both Brooks's and White's for failing to meet his obligations. That is why he had to leave London in such a hurry."

"Oh, dear, now you have disappointed me." Caroline giggled. "I quite thought he had come out here for love of me."

"For love of your money, more like. Now more than ever he needs to make sure you do not win that wretched wager. Lord Letton refuses to pay any more of his debts and says D'Arcy will have to wait until he is dead and buried before he gets another penny. Unfortunately, that does not nullify your wager, for he will then inherit both money and title, but in the meantime he is apparently quite hard pressed and your money will help to tide him over very nicely."

Caroline made the excuse that she was tired and was going upstairs to rest. She did not wish to pursue the conversation as she was in no mood to explain that she had almost decided to let Sir D'Arcy have his way. She sat in the rocking chair her uncle had bought for her and watched the boys and little Prissy snowballing each other. She only wished that she too could throw off all her cares and run down to join them. If only she had someone to talk to about her troubles, and if only that someone could be Pierce Chinery. But as she thought about it, she knew that was a hopeless proposition, for he was the last person in the world she could tell all the things that were running through her mind at that moment.

11

By the time Christmas Day arrived, Caroline had sufficiently recovered to join in some of the children's party games. Miss Fairchild and her brother were heartily pleased to see her looking more like herself than she had done for many weeks. Although, as Eliza remarked to her brother, Caroline had lost a great deal of her sparkle, and it was not all due to her recent bout of ill health.

By the new year she was well enough to go for a short sleigh ride and watch them fox hunting on the lake. It bore little resemblance to the hunts she had attended back home. The huntsmen were dressed in a motley array of bright woollens and furs, and the lady riders wore coarse woollen stockings over their shoes. Some were on horseback, and others, like Caroline, followed the chase in their carioles. But like anywhere else in the world, as soon as a captive fox was let loose on the ice of the bay, the hounds were after it in full cry.

As a horsewoman, Caroline had enjoyed the thrill of the chase, the feeling of the sun and wind on her face as she went sailing over hedges and ditches, giving little thought to the reasons for her actions. Today, however, her sympathy was for the fox, and she hated seeing it slipping and sliding as it tried to run over the ice. She begged her uncle to take her home, much to D'Arcy Letton's disgust. He had been one of the main organizers of the affair and was anxious to show his prowess. Caroline wondered what Pierce would say to it. She had asked him once if he enjoyed hunting, and he had said that, like the Indians, he believed that man should hunt only for food, never for sport alone.

She repeated this to Letton next time he came to call

upon her and said she had come to agree with it. "My dear Caroline," he had replied in the slightly patronizing tone he adopted whenever he was criticized in any way or was speaking to people he considered his inferiors, "You're beginning to go native. You really mustn't let these colonials influence you, especially a damn Yankee like Pierce Chinery. That man is an absolute outsider. I can't think why you tolerate him at all."

"Because he has many qualities that I've come to admire in a man, D'Arcy," Caroline had snapped back.

"Possibly"—Letton smiled sardonically—"but I was speaking as a gentleman. Don't tell me that you've come to prefer your men dirty and stinking of sweat, for if you have, it will be my duty and my pleasure to reeducate you." He flicked an imaginary speck of dust from the velvet lapels of his blue broadcloth coat. Caroline noted how white and soft his hands were, compared to the captain's lean, strong brown ones. Of the two, she much preferred the latter, for D'Arcy's hands lacked character; they were good for little else but holding cards or a duelling pistol.

Mistaking her glance for one of admiration, he reached out and took her hand in his. "Why don't you admit defeat and give up this silly charade, my dear. You don't belong out here, and it is ruining both your health and your complexion. Cry 'quits' and let me take you home, back to civilization."

His hands felt like cold dead fish, and Caroline shivered at his touch. Letton's eyes hardened, and he said tersely, "Don't repulse me Caroline, for we are fated to spend the rest of our lives together, like it or not."

"Only if I fail to keep my side of the bargain," Caroline said with as much bravado as she could muster. In her weakened state she felt no match for Letton, yet she felt she could not go through with her recent resolve to let him become her husband and her lover.

"Yes, but don't try to find comfort in that. Time is on my side, not yours. You may only have another four months to go, but they are the worst of the year. What is more, my lady, you should remember that a gambler always plays to win, and I have no intention of losing this game, whatever you may wish."

After Sir D'Arcy had left her that evening, Caroline cried herself to sleep. She felt that she was between the devil and the deep blue sea and there was no one to whom she could turn for help. She confided in Anna the next time her friend came to call, having no wish to disturb her aunt's happiness so near to her wedding.

"It is a pity you let D'Arcy Letton know of your regard for Pierce—"

"But I didn't. I merely remarked that Pierce Chinery did not approve of hunting for pleasure," Caroline hastened to interrupt.

"You didn't need to. One has only to look at your face whenever you mention Pierce's name to know how you feel about him, and Letton's no fool. We were at the Kendalls' for dinner last evening, and he was doing his best to incite my father-in-law to take action against the many Americans in our midst, saying they were only bent on causing trouble and should never be allowed to hold political office, no matter how much they affirmed their loyalty to the crown."

"You think his remarks were directed at Pierce?" Caroline asked anxiously.

"I know they were, for Chad challenged him on the subject, and he immediately cited Pierce as an example. They got into quite a bitter argument, and unfortunately, Mr. Kendall senior sided against his own son on the question."

"Oh, dear God, I do hope I haven't made things difficult for Pierce." Caroline was wretched with remorse. "There is so little I can do. Whatever I say now will only aggravate the matter."

"Try not to fret about it," Anna said comfortingly. "I would not have mentioned it, but I felt you should know the situation and so avoid any further mention of Pierce when Letton is present."

"Oh, Anna . . ." Caroline began to weep. "I seem to be such a clown, I'm always doing or saying such stupid things. Is there nothing I can do to put matters straight? It makes me feel that I should go back to England as soon as possible to avoid doing any further harm."

"Nonsense! Whatever happens now, you have to stay until the year is out, come hell or high water. At least you have come to realize that marriage to Letton is quite out of the question."

"I know," Caroline agreed. "I've decided I would prefer to die an old maid than be married to that . . . that fiend. I think I will instruct Hannah that I am not at home to Sir D'Arcy Letton in future."

"I wouldn't do that," Anna replied wisely. "He is a vicious man, and it will only cause further trouble."

But without any action on Lady Caroline's part, trouble came. A few days later, on the very eve of Eliza Fairchild's marriage to the count, young Patrick Ryan arrived back in town. He, with Daniel Logan, had been left in charge of the Chinery estate while Pierce was away. At first Caroline thought he had come to visit his mother, but he asked to see her uncle and Chad, who had come with Anna to spend the night with the Count de la Fayre.

When he emerged from the library with the two men, Patrick's face was ashen and his eyes wide with fear. He was glad to obey Stephen's instructions, and hurried off to the kitchen to see his mother and get something to eat. It was easy to see from the expression on Mr. Fairchild's face that something was gravely wrong, and Caroline had never seen Chad look so angry since the day Oliver Rowlands had insulted Anna.

"For pity's sake, tell us that's wrong," Caroline and her aunt cried in unison.

"A great deal, I'm afraid," Mr. Fairchild said, drawing them into the privacy of the library. "Young Ryan tells us that last night a crowd of young ruffians attacked Captain Chinery's place and burned down his barn. Some of the settlers came to his and Logan's assistance, and they managed to frighten them off before they did any more damage, but most of his harvest has been lost."

"Yes! And what is even more distressing," Chad said, "there are political overtones to it."

"How can you tell?" Miss Fairchild asked.

"Ryan says they were calling out for the Yankees to go back where they came from and that Chinery wouldn't be the only one to suffer. They seemed somewhat taken aback when they discovered that the captain was not at home, and as soon as Logan started firing his gun in the air, they quickly dispersed." Stephen Fairchild gave his sister a curious look, which she was quick to interpret.

"You think that the perpetrators of this outrage had been put up to it by a third party?"

"Exactly," Stephen replied. "It is quite obvious that their hearts were not in it, wouldn't you agree, Kendall?"

"They were nothing but a gang of drunken hooligans recruited from the local taverns. They have no interest in politics, and they'll do anything for money. I've no doubt many of them are on quite friendly terms with Pierce and would let him buy them a mug of ale if they were to meet tomorrow." Chad's normally open, happy face looked grim. "I've every intention of going down to the taverns tonight to find out who is at the bottom of all this."

Anna clutched at her husband's arm. "Chad, do be careful. They far outnumber you."

"Don't worry." He patted her hand reassuringly. "You forget I'm a Kendall, and that name carries some weight in these parts. It's about time that I wielded some of the power attached to it."

Caroline had detached herself from the group and was standing looking down into the fire "There is no need for anyone to go," she said quietly. "For I already know who is at the bottom of this."

"Maybe, Lady Caroline, but we have to have proof."

"Even if it involves a member of your own family?"

"Even more, if that is the case," Chad answered curtly. "Pierce is my best friend, and I have no intention of standing by while his whole future goes up in flames."

"Where is Captain Chinery?" Miss Eliza cut in. "In his last letter to Stephen he said he would be home for my wedding."

"And I've no doubt that is his intention, for I've always found Pierce to be a man of his word. But there was a bad snowstorm in Kingston a few days ago, and I imagine the Danforth Road is in a hazardous condition for travellers. I'm sure he will be with us before long."

Caroline persuaded her aunt to retire early, as she had to look her best for the morrow's ceremony. She stayed up with Anna and waited for Chad and Mr. Fairchild to return. Stephen had insisted on accompanying Kendall on their tour of the taverns in search of information.

"How right you were, Anna, when you said that Letton was a vicious man. I only wish I had been more circumspect in my conversation. Where will this top? . . . Heaven alone knows, unless I agree to go back with him."

"Don't even think of such a thing," Anna said angrily, although her face was pale and Caroline guessed that she was worried about Chad. It was midnight before the men returned, and then, to Caroline's great joy, they brought Pierce Chinery along with them. It turned out that they had met him earlier and he had eagerly accompanied them as soon as he heard the news.

They were all too tired and angry to discuss it with the ladies, and demanded that for the sake of their health they should both retire to their beds immediately. Chad was anxious about his wife because of her delicate condition, while Mr. Fairchild said Caroline should go because she was still far from being fully recovered.

"I'm perfectly all right, Uncle Stephen," his niece protested, clinging shakily to Pierce's hand. The captain had just crossed the room to greet her and as yet had not had an opportunity to speak other than a general greeting. "Go to bed, Caroline," he said, looking down at her. "For heaven's sake, do as you're told for once without arguing. I thought during my absence you might have mended your ways, instead of which you have been causing everyone a great deal of anguish over your health." He spoke gruffly, but his expression was troubled as he took in all the ravages her recent fever had left behind—her face, drawn and pale in the candlelight, and her gown hanging about a figure much too thin. He raised her hand to his lips and kissed it gently. "Look at this," he said, turning it over in his own strong one. "It is nothing but skin and bone, not worth throwing to a dog. Be off with you, and not another word."

His manner was so stern and masterful that Caroline could do nothing else but obey. But as she lay in bed and listened to the murmur of voices from the room below, she felt relieved to know that he was back, for with him had come an aura of strength, and she felt the life returning within her. Caroline knew now that she loved Pierce Chinery beyond any doubt, and even if she had to spend the rest of her life in the wilderness, she would do so rather than be parted from him again. What a fool she had been not to have admitted it before, when she was sure with a little encouragement from her he would have spoken out. Now there was no telling what he might do. She had so often protested against the idea of staying in Canada and had let him see there were so many things of which she did not approve, who could blame him if he had turned his attention elsewhere? Caroline would have no peace until she could find out where she stood with him, even if she had to ask him outright, unladylike and indelicate though that may be.

The next day everyone did his best to appear happy for

Miss Fairchild's sake, but even she wore a gloomy countenance while they were seated at breakfast. "Were you able to discover who was at the bottom of this dastardly affair?" she questioned her brother. He was the only one of the three men present, Chad and Pierce having spent the night at the Count de la Fayre's, Stephen Fairchild's old house on King Street.

Mr. Fairchild shook his head. "There were hints, nods and winks, and a great deal of freeloading as far as drinks were concerned, but no one was ready to speak up. In fact, I was left with the unhappy impression that there is yet more mischief afoot. If that is the case, no one will say anything. They would be cutting their own throats, for undoubtedly they are being paid handsomely for their trouble."

"I am in no doubt as to who is behind it," Eliza rapped back. "D'Arcy Letton is the man you want."

"I think we are all aware of that," Stephen Fairchild said, frowning at his sister and casting a glance in Caroline's direction. "The trouble is, we have to prove it before we can take any action."

Caroline had left her breakfast untouched. She was having a great deal of difficulty in holding back her tears. That all this should have come to a head on her aunt's wedding day and that she held herself mainly responsible was almost more than she could bear. She made the excuse that she wanted to lay out the lavender silk gown and bonnet that her aunt was to wear for the ceremony and rushed upstairs. She did not show her face again until Anna came to say that the few guests had assembled and Miss Fairchild was ready to go down.

Anna was looking lovely; the ruby-red gown she had bought in New York brought out the colour of her dark hair, but the face beneath it was nearly as pale as Caroline's. "How is Pierce this morning?" Caroline asked.

Anna busied herself straightening the cluster of green feathers on Caroline's oyster-coloured velvet bonnet and did not reply. "What is the matter, Anna? . . . What are you keeping from me?" Caroline persisted as she saw Anna's expression reflected in the mirror.

"I think that you should wait for Pierce to tell you himself, for I have only heard it at secondhand from Chad."

"What is it, Anna?" Caroline begged. "I am not prepared for any more shocks, so please tell me. If it is that bad, I will at least have time to prepare myself."

"I don't know what to make of it," Anna said, her own

eyes brimming with tears. "And Chad is far too upset to speculate. He merely said that Pierce told him last night that he had come back to arrange for the sale of his property, that he planned to get married and was going away. . . . That's all Chad could get out of him and they were both so tired and had so much on their minds that I did not think it right to worry them further."

Caroline thought she was going to faint, but they heard Joseph Fairchild strike up the wedding music on the piano. With a tremendous effort she pulled herself together and went out with Anna, to accompany her aunt downstairs to where the Count de la Fayre was waiting with the rest of the assembly.

The wedding ceremony itself was short and simple. Unfortunately, the few words the clergyman decided to say in conclusion proved to take the best part of half an hour. He delivered his little homily with a great number of elevations and depressions of the voice and accompanied this with long closings of the eyes. At any other time Caroline would have been suffocated with laughter. Even now she had to smile as she caught Pierce's eye and saw that he was having a job not to laugh. But then, apart from the trouble out at the farm, he had plenty to smile about, for was he not going to be married? She wondered what magic the young woman possessed that she could make him agree to give up his beloved land for her.

For some reason unknown to either herself or Anna, Chad and Stephen Fairchild between them had persuaded the count and his bride to go out to de la Fayre's old home for a few days. Chad said he had some business in town and that he and Anna would look after the place on King Street. It was not until after the couple had left in company with some of the count's old neighbours, who had promised to see they arrived safely at the old log house, that the girls were told what it was all about.

"I did not wish to darken your aunt's happiness any more than necessary," Stephen Fairchild told his niece. "But one thing we did learn last night was that they are planning to hold a shivaree, and the way things are at the moment, I do not think there will be much goodwill about it. Anna will sleep here with you tonight, while I go round to keep Chad and Pierce company."

"No," Anna protested. "I saw Chad cleaning his pistol this morning; he did not think I had noticed. If you are expecting that kind of trouble, I must be at my husband's side."

"And I heartily agree with Anna," Caroline said sharply. "I have my own small pistol, which I always carry when travelling, and I have every intention of being at your side, for Aunt Eliza would never forgive me if anything should happen. She will never believe I wasn't in your conspiracy."

The ladies remained adamant in spite of Pierce and Chad's pleas and commands. "I always understood that women were supposed to be the weaker sex," Pierce said, having given in reluctantly. "But I now understand why the devils were so pleased to be rid of the farmer's wife. I have never met such stubbornness in all my life, and I hope never to do so again."

"You will," Caroline said bitterly, "now you've decided to take a wife yourself."

Pierce raised an eyebrow and looked at her questioningly. However, if she had hoped to provoke him into saying more on the matter, she was to be sadly disappointed. He gave her one of his slow tantalizing smiles that always provoked her, because she knew he was keeping something back, and said, "Yes, ma'am, no doubt you're right."

Immediately it began to grow dusk they left the house on Front Street, Chad and Pierce riding and Mr. Fairchild driving the ladies in the cariole. After supper the gentlemen retired to the library with their pipes and some imported wine Pierce had brought back with him, while Caroline and Anna sat in front of the parlour fire and tried to concentrate on their sewing. Their nerves were frayed and they started up at the least sound, darting to peek through the shutters they had been forbidden to open. Caroline kept her reticule with the little pearl-handled pistol close at her side and did her best to feel brave, although her heart was pounding against her ribs.

It was a clear, frosty night and every sound echoed along the street. Every now and then they would hear the sound of sleigh bells in the distance, and they became tense wondering who was approaching and what would be the outcome of the night's events. Caroline got up and started pacing the room, stopping every once in a while to peer out at the ice-covered street. Suddenly she caught her breath and reached into her bag.

"What is it?" Anna said, joining her at the window.

"I think they are here," Caroline said in a whisper. "I

saw some dark shadows flit across the garden. But it's strange they are not making a sound."

"They will do that sometimes," Anna replied. "They keep quiet until everyone has assembled, and then all hell will suddenly break loose." She had scarcely finished speaking when her words became painfully true. There was such a din outside that the girls flew into each other's arms in terror. When they had recovered sufficiently to peek out again, they saw a crowd of twenty or more rough-looking characters prancing around the house. Some were dressed up to look like Indians, others had sacks over their heads with holes cut in them for their eyes. They beat a constant noise upon their assorted kettles and drums, bells tied to their ankles and wrists, yahooing while they capered and banged on the windows with tin plates.

"Good grief! How long will they keep this up?"

"Heaven only knows," Anna rejoined. "They will sometimes come back several nights in a row."

"Thank God Aunt Eliza isn't here to see."

Stephen Fairchild came in just then to see they were all right. "Where is Chad?" Anna asked.

"It's all right, my dear, he and I are just going to the door to see if they will go away if we treat them. We will try a moderate approach first. If that doesn't work, then we shall have to take more drastic measures." He patted a pistol hidden beneath his coat.

"And where is Pierce?" Caroline asked, catching her breath in anticipation of the answer.

"Pierce will be all right, rest assured," her uncle replied.

"That doesn't answer my question, uncle. Where is he?"

"He left some time ago. He borrowed one of my Indian masks and went out to mingle with the crowd. He said that was the only way to find out who is behind all this."

Caroline and Anna stood back in the shadow of the doorway and listened as Chad and Mr. Fairchild tried to gain the attention of the mob, but there was no silencing them; even when Chad fetched a lantern so they might see his face. Once when they did quieten and stood huddled together in their ridiculous disguises waiting to see what the two men facing them would do, there came a loud furor of crashing tins and wooden rattles from the back. And above it all, Caroline was certain she heard, among others, D'Arcy Letton's voice egging them on. They renewed their jeers and taunts, and one or two picked up handfuls of snow and hurled them at the steps. Slowly the dark mass began to advance again toward Stephen Fairchild and Chad Kendall; they knew that Fairchild was a peaceful man who would do anything to avoid trouble, and as for Chad, they had long dismissed him as weak.

Caroline heard the click as the two men cocked their guns, and she slipped out behind them with Anna clinging to her skirts. She held the little pistol in her hand, which was trembling like a leaf. A heavily built figure on the fringe of the crowd stepped forward into the light from the lantern, and doffing the sacking mask he wore over his head, bowed mockingly. There was no mistaking the coarse features of Caleb Wallis. Caroline caught her breath; she had not realized that he was free again. But now she was sure the Kendalls and Letton were behind it, otherwise he would never have dared to show his face. No doubt he was currying favour with them—or was it just from his own consuming hatred of all she stood for?

Stephen Fairchild had been driven to the brink, and as the first men reached the bottom step, he was afraid for the safety of the two girls. He raised his weapon to fire a warning shot over the heads of the crowd, but before he could do so, the deafening sound of a musket rang out through the cold air. It was accompanied by the clatter of horses' hooves galloping over the frozen road, and Pierce on his great black stallion cleared the fence and ended up in the midst of the throng.

The speed and fierceness of his assault brought them to their senses, and they started to fall back through the open gates, some of those nearest to him cringing away from the lash of the thick leather whip he was flourishing. He drove them back to the other side of the street before dismounting and striding across to a small gathering of men waiting in the shadow of a nearby tree.

"Come out, Letton!" Pierce called in a voice that would have put thunder to shame. "I'm calling you out, Letton, if you're man enough."

A tall slim figure stepped out and pulled off the corn mask he had been wearing. "At your service, Captain Chinery," he said with an arrogant bow. And Caroline, watching, saw the cruel smirk of satisfaction on Sir D'Arcy's face in the pale light of the winter moon. "I take it your seconds will be calling upon me in the morning?" There was no mistaking the note of triumph in his voice; it was for this that he had been waiting.

"Damn you and damn your seconds! We'll make our arrangements here and now. I'll meet you at seven o'clock out on the peninsula. And may God have mercy on your soul, for you'll get none from me."

"It will give me the greatest pleasure to send you to hell before another night has passed," Letton replied.

"We shall see," Pierce growled back at him. "Now, call your scum off and fight me like a man rather than hound innocent folk like the predator you are."

But there was no need for D'Arcy Letton to say another word. As silently as they had come, the crowd had melted away, leaving the two men facing each other in the moonlight.

"Until seven tomorrow morning," D'Arcy said; then, bowing again, he turned on his heel and walked away, and there was only the sound of his boots crunching the snow.

As she heard Pierce issue his challenge, Caroline hastily clapped her hand over her mouth to stifle a scream. Anna put her arm around her, and the two women clung together in the shadow of the porch, dreading what they knew was bound to transpire. No man of honour could refuse to fight in such a case, and all too frequently it ended in at least one death. Often too the so-called victor would die from an infected wound. Duelling had been forbidden in many parts, but here in the New World there was as yet no firmly established system of law and order, and what there was tended to turn a blind eye, especially where gentlemen were concerned. Only in street fights was the constable willing to make an arrest and bring the culprit before a magistrate, so there would be no help from that quarter.

Pierce stood alone, a tall dark figure in his heavy cloak, casting a long shadow on the crisp white snow. He waited until D'Arcy and his friends had reached their horses and were riding off down the road before he turned toward the house. Only then did the little group waiting at the door come to life. Caroline rushed forward and grabbed the captain's arm.

"Pierce, for the love of God," she pleaded, "Letton is one of the best marksmen in England. He has already killed three men, to my knowledge."

"I had to," he said, drawing her into the shelter of his

cloak, for she was shivering pitifully, but more from fear than cold. "It's what he wanted. Nothing less would have silenced him."

"Yes, there is one thing that would stay his hand," Caroline said softly.

Pierce stopped, and grasping her by the shoulders, turned her round so that he could look down into her eyes. "No," he said firmly. "Not even that, for I will never have it said I hid behind a woman's skirts."

Caroline dropped her head. "I was thinking of your bride, whoever she may be. I would not wish such grief on any woman." There was no time to say more, for the others had joined them, and together they all went back into the house. The men looked grave and the ladies left them talking of weapons and the like while they prepared some food and wine. Caroline set the tray before them in the parlour while Anna threw more logs upon the fire. There was little else they could do for the moment.

"I think you should go to bed, Anna," Chad said to his wife. "I shall stay with Pierce until the morning."

"I think it well if both the ladies retired. This business is not suitable for them to hear," Pierce said, looking directly at Caroline. Then, getting up, he came across and took both her hands in his. "Never fear, I shall return to provoke you yet again, my lady." For a second his grey eyes gleamed with impish laughter.

"But D'Arcy Letton—" Caroline started again to voice her fears regarding his opponent's skill.

Pierce guessed what was coming and shook his head reproachfully. "I'm sorry you have so little faith in a poor colonial, ma'am. But don't forget I was a soldier once, and I do know one end of a gun from t'other." He gave her hands a final squeeze, then turned her around and set her face toward the door.

12

Stephen Fairchild drove his niece back to the house on Front Street and told her to go to bed and get some rest. He was going to take a pair of duelling pistols round to Pierce for his consideration before going to see the doctor and arrange for him to be present the following morning. He did not say this to Caroline, but she knew the ritual of the duel too well to be in any doubt.

She went up to her room but did not attempt to go to bed; sleep was the last thing she could hope for that night. Instead she sat by the window looking out across the snow to where the lighthouse stood stark and foreboding on the tip of the peninsula. Within a few hours a scene would be played out there that could change the course of her entire life. Caroline was too numb with misery to be conscious of her emotions; she could not think of what might lie beyond the next morning.

As soon as the red fingers of dawn began to streak the sky, she rose and changed into a brown velvet riding habit. Then, after setting a fur cap on her amber curls and wrapping herself round in a heavy cloak, she stole downstairs to saddle the little bay mare. She did not know whether her uncle had already left or even if he had returned that night, but she was anxious to be away before anyone should see her. Keeping under cover of the trees as far as possible, she made her way toward the peninsula.

News of such an event travels fast in a small town offering little entertainment. Already small groups of people were wending their way toward the duelling ground. Caroline shuddered at the ghoulish delight they were taking at the morning's sport. As she drew near the bleak scene, she could make out the tall figure of Pierce Chinery, with Chad and her uncle beside him, and a short distance away, Letton, with several of the Kendalls at his back. She tied her horse to a tree branch, and pulling the hood of her cloak over her head to hide her face, she lost herself in the crowd of onlookers.

It did not worry her that it was not considered seemly for a lady of good breeding to be present at such events. Her only fear was that Pierce might see her and be put off his stride. Clasping her hands until her knuckles were white with pain, she watched as her uncle and John Kendall made the customary attempt to reconcile the principals. It was a part of the ritual to which no one paid much heed, as all present knew that neither Chinery or Letton was prepared to apologize. Chad presented the case containing the duelling pistols to each man in turn; then their seconds stepped forward and took their cloaks. Caroline saw the soft white flecks of snow falling from the grey sky, settling on Pierce's fair curls as the two men stood back to back, a cruel smile of triumph on Letton's face.

Her lips moved in silent prayer as the throng around her chanted out the paces. Seven . . . eight . . . nine . . . Caroline closed her eyes; she could bear no more. But as she did so, a shot rang out a moment before the count of ten. A gasp went up from the crowd. One of the principals had broken the strict code of honour and fired before the count was finished. Her eyes flew wide with fear, but it was some seconds before she could bring herself to look at the ground ahead. When she did, she saw Pierce standing, his gun aimed at Letton's heart. Everyone held his breath waiting for the fatal shot, knowing nothing could save Sir D'Arcy now.

Caroline saw the agonized look on the captain's face. He was well within his rights to kill his opponent where he stood, and many would think him less of a man were he not to do so. But Caroline knew it would cost him as much to kill a man in cold blood as it would to walk way. The dilemma had to be resolved.

"No, Pierce!" she cried, breaking from the cover of the crowd. "You are not a murderer. I would not have you live with such a deed for all the world."

Pierce hesitated for a moment without taking his eyes from Letton's face. "Not when one shot from me would mean your freedom?" he said, while Chad hurried forward to put a restraining hand on Caroline's arm.

"No, not even for that. You are too much of a man to destroy life wantonly. Your spirit would never know a moment's peace. I love you far too much for that!"

She sensed the stir her words had caused amongst the

group surrounding them, but she no longer cared what people might think of her; all life's pettiness was washed away in the flood of her concern. Slowly Pierce raised his arm and fired into the air. D'Arcy Letton smiled and began to turn away, but Pierce, throwing his weapon aside, sprang on him like a maddened dog.

"No, Letton, our quarrel isn't settled yet. We'll forget that you're a gentleman and fight this man to man." Chinery's first blow felled D'Arcy, and he crouched on the ground, blood streaming from his nose. For the first time his face showed fear. He knew he was no match with his fists, and the rage on Pierce's face told him he could expect no quarter there.

Chinery stood towering over him, his feet astride, ready to land another blow. "Get up and fight, or admit now that you are licked and that all debts are paid, for Caroline belongs to me. I'll not see you live to take her in your arms."

He grasped Letton by the collar and dragged him to his feet, a wretched whimpering bundle of fear. He mumbled something to the captain, who dragged him across to where Caroline was standing. "Tell her," Pierce said, throwing Letton at her feet, "and let everyone hear you say you consider the wager between you paid." D'Arcy Letton had no choice but to do as he was bid.

The crowd, deprived of their sport, had already begun to trek back toward the town while Letton and his party stole away. Caleb Wallis shambled across and flung the little gold fob watch at her feet. "You dropped this, m'lady," he said before turning away.

"An oafish fellow, but honest," Pierce said, stooping to pick it up and hand it to her.

Caroline took it but said nothing. She wondered why Caleb had chosen to return it. Perhaps he had been unable to find a safe market and was afraid of being caught with it; perhaps time and experience had wrought a change in him, as it had in her—who could tell? Watching him go, Caroline doubted it; the flaws in his character ran too deep, and it would not take much for them to surface again. But she was sure of herself at last. Life without Pierce would be no life at all. And if it meant yielding her future to this as-yet-untamed land, then so be it, as long as he was by her side.

"Now," Pierce said, taking Caroline in his arms, "we'll have no more nonsense, for I have always intended that you should be my wife." Caroline buried her head against his broad chest and wept with relief and joy. When at last she looked up, they were quite alone on the silent shore.

"Come," he said, his arm about her as he drew her toward the shelter of the trees. "If you take cold again . . ."

"I know"—Caroline smiled softly—"you would not get a wooden nickel for me."

In the shadow of the dark pines standing like sentinels against the frozen vastness of the lake, he kissed her with all the passion he had shown the first night on the garrison hill. "Kissing cousins?" she whispered demurely as he paused for breath.

"Cousins, be damned!" he said fiercely. "I've no desire to bed my cousin!"

The warmth of his body had brought her back to life, and the colour began to return to her cheeks. Her eyes were shining as she looked up at him and said, "But I understood you were selling up . . . that you were about to be married. . . . So I assumed that it was to your English cousin."

Pierce laughed merrily to see the questions in her eyes. "You must get out of the habit of being wrong; it takes so much of my time converting you." He heaved a sigh of mock despair. "But it will be my burden in life which I feel compelled to carry, for no other man could manage you."

"Then you will not be leaving Canada?"

"Now, there for once you are right." He fell silent for a moment and kicked at some dead branches with his foot.

"Why?" Caroline asked.

"Because this wilderness is not yet ready for a lady to live in, and I want Lady Caroline Fairchild for my wife."

"More than this land with all the promise that it holds?"

"Yes," Pierce replied, looking down into her eyes. "More than all that. I realized when I saw the toll it was taking on you that you were not meant to tear a living from this harsh country, beautiful as it may be. That is why I went to see my father. He is heir to the Earl of Tarn, although he has always sworn he would never claim the title when it falls to him, good republican that he is. But I needed it for you. If we are to live in England, then my wife must have the rank in society to which she is accustomed."

Caroline's hand stole up to caress his face. "You would do all that for me?"

"Yes," he said, drawing her close to him again. She kissed him gently, savouring the joy of all that true love could mean. Then, pushing him away, she jumped up on her little mare, which had been standing patiently tethered to a tree.

"How very unfortunate." She laughed. "I cannot see much coming from this marriage, for I intend to stay—I'll not let any of your devils frighten me away."

Like lightning Pierce pulled her down and tumbled her beneath him in the snow. "And what does that mean?" he demanded.

"That I intend to be a farmer's wife."

"And breed his sons to till the land?"

"And his daughters to bake his bread."

"Then let us begin," he said, pulling her to her feet. "For there is little else we can do until the spring."

"Pierce Chinery," she replied, blushing becomingly. "I always knew that you were incorrigible. No gentleman would have said such a thing. What would the good citizens of York think? At least wait for the blessing of the church."

They mounted their horses and stood with them reined in looking out over the harbour and the lake beyond, and for a moment he was serious again. "Do you really think that you can face the rigours of this land?" he asked.

"With you beside me, I can face the world and all it brings," she answered.

"It is a magnificent country for our children to inherit. Just think of the life we can build for them here." They turned their horses toward the town. "One day soon," Pierce said, pointing inland, "this town of York will match any city in the world."

"And to make sure of it, you will become governor of Upper Canada," Caroline teased.

"I don't know about that . . . I haven't quite made up my mind . . . but if I did, do you know the first thing I should do?"

"No," Caroline said, recognizing the mischief in his eyes.

"I'd give York back its name."

"What do you mean?" she asked with some surprise.

"Didn't you know?" Pierce said. "The Hurons used to call it Toronto—a place of meeting!"

ABOUT THE AUTHOR

NELLA BENSON is making her literary debut with *The Reckless Wager,* thus adding another element to an impressive list of credentials. Ms. Benson has taken degrees from both the University of London, England and the University of Windsor, Ontario. In addition, she has won a gold medal in public speaking from the London Academy of Music and Dramatic Art. At various points in her career, Ms. Benson has been on the staffs of several major universities, has pursued a business career, has been a scriptwriter and has produced and directed in both television and theatre. She has also lectured extensively throughout Canada and England. Ms. Benson is presently living in Ontario.